WALTE

The Wanderer between the Two Worlds

An Experience of War

Translated by Brian Murdoch

This edition first published by Rott Publishing 2014

First published under the title *Der Wanderer zwischen beiden Welten*, Beck, Munich, 1918

Translation and afterword copyright © Brian Murdoch {2014}

© Rott Publishing {2014}

ISBN: **9781520194653**

www.rottpublishing.com

CONTENTS

Walter Flex, *c* 1915
Staatsbibliothek zu Berlin

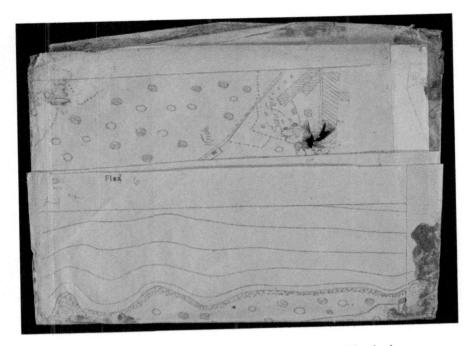

This map was found in Flex's bag after he was shot. The hole was probably made by the bullet that killed him in October 1917. Staatsbibliothek zu Berlin

The cover of the first edition of *The Wanderer between the Two Worlds*

The security of a throne is founded upon poetry
Gneisenau

To the memory of my dear friend

Ernst Wurche

Volunteer, 3rd Lower Saxon Infantry-Regiment 30;

Lieutenant, 3rd Lower Alsace Infantry-Regiment 138

A stormy early spring night spread over the war-wounded woodlands of Lorraine, where a hail of iron had, over the months, marked and stripped every tree-trunk. I had joined as a volunteer, and lay on the shell-ploughed ground of this wood, as I had done for a hundred nights before, on sentry-duty, staring with eyes stung by the wind into the flickering light and dark of that stormy night, through which searchlights roved restlessly over the French and German trenches. The roar of the night's attack rolled noisily over me. Unknown voices filled the vibrating air. The wind whistled and sang, shrill and lamenting, over the tops of helmets and the barrels of rifles, and high above the massed troops of the enemy, migrating grey geese flew northwards, their cries cutting the air.

The flickering and fading brightness of the Very lights as they went up illuminated again and again in stark suddenness the lumpy outlines of hunched figures, covered up, like me, in coats and tarpaulins, a chain of lookouts, pressed down along the line of our wire in hollows and chalk-bunkers. The lookout-chain of our Silesian regiment stretched from the Bois de Chevaliers down to the Bois des Vérines, and the migrating flock of wild geese flew over us all like ghosts. Even though I couldn't see the lines I was writing in the dark, I wrote a few verses on a scrap of paper:

> Wild geese rush through the night-time air
> Northwards with rasping cry.
> Uneasy flight! beware, beware,
> In a world where all can die.
>
> Fly onwards though the world's night-skies,
> Grey wandering squadrons all!

Light flickers, there are battle cries,
War rages, rises, falls.

Rush on, soar on, army of grey,
Rush northwards to the sea
When you fly south again some day,
Where and what shall we be!

We too are an army clad in grey,
We move at the Kaiser's call,
And if we must forever stay,
Sound our Amen in the fall.

While I was writing this in the Bois des Chevaliers, over in the woods at Vérines a twenty-year old theology student, a volunteer like me, was also on sentry-duty. At that time neither of us knew of the other. However, when he, several months later, came across those verses in my war-diary, he recalled very clearly that night and the migrating flocks of wild geese that had flown over us both. We had both watched them with the same thoughts. And at the very same time we each received from the darkness of the trenches behind us an operational command with orders to report to the regimental orderly-room at midnight, prepared to move out. As we left, our weary and yet strangely wakeful senses became aware again of the melancholy beauty of the bare, grey hills and hollows, the chalk of which looks dead, strange and heavy in the moonlight, and the obscure, grey loneliness of the shell-ravaged and abandoned stone dwellings...

In the regimental orderly room we learned that we were to be sent with twenty other volunteers back to Germany, to take an officers' training course at a camp in Posen.

Early the following day our little troop gathered on the pitted village street between the bombed-out church and the priest's house with the war-graves beside it. At the same time another group was due to leave the place, a troop of men who had worked in slaughterhouses, and who had been taken out of the ranks to be employed back home. While we were standing in columns in front of the priest's house waiting for the order to move off, a major came towards us and shouted out while still at a distance: "Are you lot the butchers, then?" and a chorus of indignant and amused voices shouted back: "No sir, we're the officer candidates!" While the major, with dark mutterings, strode past us on the continued search for his butchers, I glanced quite by accident into a pair of strikingly beautiful, light-grey eyes. They belonged to the man next to me, and were sparkling with laughter. We looked at each other and were brought together by the delight in one of those little, harmlessly comical events that made up so much of our existence as volunteer soldiers. I thought: what pure, clear eyes the young man has! and I took note of his name when the regimental clerk called it out. "Ernst Wurche." "Here!" Well, I thought, that's good, you and I are going the same way...

A few hours later our little troop was going down the inclines of the Côtes Lorraine from Hâtonchatel to Vigneuilles. The steepness of the downhill march and the fresh air, full of dew and sunlight made you put your head back without realising it, and before long a song was fluttering over the little grey troop like a bright and cheerful banner. "Onwards, the air is fresh and fine, just idling is a waste! See how the sun in glory shines, of heaven it's a taste." How long has it been since we sang that? The young student at my side had a voice that was as clear and pure as his eyes. Anyone who sings that well must be good to

3

talk to, I thought, while he expressed through the song his unfeigned delight in the newly awakened joys of rambling…

The road descended ever more steeply onto the broad flatland of Lorraine. At a sharp turn halfway down we found ourselves looking backwards, up to the church at Hâtonchatel, bathed in the red light of dawn and the early mists, and onto its Gothic decorations the young sun was breaking through in bright streaks, lighting up the shell-shot houses all around it; and then the hillside cemetery, over whose grey walls life was bursting forth in the fresh green bushes with hundreds of slender twigs, festooned with silvery, shining threads and with swelling hazel catkins. The further down we went, the more majestically there rose over the valley and the dewy vine-slopes the ruined church of Hâtonchatel, bathed in ever-stronger sunlight, a fortress of God, before which the rich land spread itself like a carpet on which great numbers of pilgrims might kneel in prayer.

Perhaps I would not have been so aware of all this had it not been for the twenty-year-old comrade at my side. He had stopped singing and was now completely absorbed in looking around as he strode along. Defiance and humility, the charm of a young man, seemed to lie like a glow upon the very bearing of his firm body, on his slim and powerful limbs, his proudly-held head and the unconventional beauty of his mouth and chin. The way he walked was springy, calm, and proclaimed a casually controlled power – we call it "striding" – and it was an even, proud stride that could become powerful in moments of danger. The way this person moved could be a game, a battle or a devotional act, depending on the circumstances. It was both prayer and pleasure. The way this slim, beautiful person in his worn grey battledress came down the hillside like a pilgrim, his bright, grey eyes shining and full of purposeful longing, made him like Zarathustra as he

4

came down from the heights, or like the Wanderer in Goethe's poem. The sun was playing in the chalk-dust kicked up by his and our boots, and the bright stone of the hill-road seemed to ring out beneath his feet...

In his movement was will and joy. He was walking from the past into the future, from his apprenticeship years into those of a master. The hills sank away behind him, where he had dug trenches with pick and spade, the woods, from which he had borne massive and heavy trunks on his willing shoulders for many an hour's journey, the villages whose streets he had kept clear with a shovel or a rake, the trenches in which he had at all hours of day or night stood on guard, and the shell-holes and dug-outs where he had for so many months lived in good comradeship with artisans, factory workers and Polish farmhands. For six months he had worn a grey uniform without pips or stripes, and he had been spared none of the hardest and most lowly duties. Now he strode down from the hills to become a leader. But he did not cast the past away like a worn-out garment, but rather he took it with him as a secret treasure. For six hard months he had done his service for the soul of his nation, something so many people talk about without really knowing it. Only someone who can carry with a full and modest heart all the misery and pitifulness of the many, their joys and their perils, can suffer with them their hunger, thirst, cold, sleeplessness, dirt and lice, danger and sickness, only to such a person does the nation open up its secret chambers, its back-rooms and its treasuries. If someone has passed with bright and kindly eyes through these chambers, then that person is certainly amongst those called to be one of the leaders of the nation. Like one aware of this in heart and head, the young volunteer soldier came down from the hills of Lorraine to become a leader and a helper of his nation. His very steps rang with it. And even

5

though men can lie and cheat in all things, they still cannot counterfeit or fake the look and voice and movement of the strong and the pure. I had not yet spoken a single word to the young student, but the look and voice and movement of the young man had already endeared themselves to me.

In the railway carriage we got into conversation. He was sitting opposite me, and he dug out of his pack a little bundle of much-read books: a little volume of Goethe, Nietzsche's *Zarathustra* and a soldiers' edition of the New Testament. "Do they all get on with each other?" I asked. He gave me a bright and slightly pugnacious look. Then he laughed. "All sorts of different types are forced into comradeship in the trenches. It's no different for books than it is for people. They can be as different as they like – they just have to be strong and honest and be able to stand up for themselves, and that's what makes for the best sort of comradeship." Without answering him, I flicked through the pages of his collection of Goethe's poems. Another soldier looked across at me and said: "I had that book in my pack when we started as well, but when do you get time to read out here?" "If you haven't got time to read," said the young student, "then you have to learn things by heart. This past winter I've learnt seventy of Goethe's poems. I can call them up as often as I like." He spoke freely and easily and without sounding in the least self-conscious or school-masterly, but his open and confident way of talking without embarrassment even about inner and essential ideas made you listen. His words were as clear as his eyes and from every one of his cleanly and honestly put-together sentences you could see before you his spiritual background.

The discussion in that compartment ranged over some aspects of the task immediately facing us. We were heading for an apprenticeship. Some thought that there would be a lot to learn, others not much in the short time we were going to have. "You don't need to be a strategist to lead a company," reckoned one of them. "Being a lieutenant means dying at the head of your men and showing them how. If you're a decent fellow, all you need to learn is a few basics." The man who said that meant it honestly, and not too long afterwards his comments came true for him somewhere in the Russian part of Poland. But his awkward and sharp way of making broad and often inappropriate statements out of the blue regularly made him, however honestly they were meant, into a target for harmless mockery. And this time, too, his comments dropped like a stone into the general chatter. Some smiled. Ernst Wurche, however, picked up the stone and in his hand it turned into a diamond. "Being a lieutenant means *living* at the head of your men and showing them how, he said, "and how to die might indeed be a part of it. A lot of people know about showing the way to die. Those words *non dolet*, it doesn't hurt, that the Roman matron once used to her hesitant husband shows how easy it is to die well, and is quite appropriate for a man and an officer. But showing the way to live is better. It is also much harder. The way we had to live together in the trenches was probably the best education for that, and nobody, I'm sure, can be a real leader if he hasn't been out here."

With that there arose a lively debate about whether it was easy or difficult to influence the thoughts and feelings of the common man. Many of them had come to grief in their attempts to educate people, and had ended up simply sticking out like a sore thumb. I can no longer recall a lot of what else was said at the time, but in fact it quite rightly pales into insignificance against one small experience recounted by the young student. "The big boys," he said with a smile, "are like children. Telling them off or forbidding them to do things isn't much use. Any game in which you don't join in isn't really a game for them.

7

Once, when there were eight of us in a dugout, one of them regularly tried to get one over on the others with dirty jokes. And for a while, this kept everyone happy. But there was one man there, a social democrat from Breslau, who was a good friend of mine; he was always the first one to notice when I didn't join in. "Ernst, old man, are you asleep too?" he would ask every time, and we both knew that the mockery was a bit shaky. I just grunted "leave me alone," or something like that. The others knew perfectly well when I didn't want to have anything to do with them, and they didn't like that at all. Then it would usually take only a little while before one of them told a joke that I laughed at as well. And then they were all pleased."

He told us this quite simply and with such an enchanting delight at the memory that you felt, without realising it, the force that his nature exercised over both coarser and finer hearts. I fully understood his "big boys", who "liked him" and who found their laughter shallow if he did not join in. Much later, in the woods around Augustów he sometimes gave me letters to read from his old comrades, with whom he regularly corresponded. Amongst them was one from that social democrat from Breslau. It opened with the words "My dear lieutenant," and in amongst all the items of news there came, somewhat abruptly, the words: "Since you left, our conversations have not improved. There are a lot of jokes that you would not laugh at, and neither do we." Even in Germany I suspect there are not many officers who would receive that kind of letter…

In the compartment of the train that took us right across Germany from Metz to Posen, I sat for many hours face to face with this comrade for whom I had rapidly come to feel great affection. There was a lot of laughter and chatter. All his words bespoke a pure, clear and composed will. The grace of the boy combined with the dignity of the man in his perfect youthfulness, and he reminded me, in his modest, self-assured and cheerful attitude to life, almost painfully of my own youngest brother, who fell in France in that first September. With these thoughts and comparisons in mind, I asked him: "weren't you a member of the *Wandervogel*, Wurche?" and with that question I had touched upon the things in his life that he most cherished! All the glory and salvation of the future of Germany seemed to him to emerge from the spirit of the *Wandervogel* movement, the young ramblers, and whenever I think of him, of a man who embodied those ideals in such a bright and pure form, then I think that he was right...

The few weeks of the training-course in the camp on the River Warthe added nothing to his essential youthfulness, and took nothing away from it. He very quickly became a corporal, a sergeant and then a lieutenant. He carried out his tasks smoothly and carefully, and he ignored as beneath him the irritations and pettiness that comes with drill-practice. On one occasion I let slip a harsh word – I no longer recall what or whom it was about. But he put his arm in mine, looked at me with his winning cheerfulness, and quoted from one of his Goethe poems:

> Wanderer, such trials and stress
> Would you try to resist?
> Whirlwinds or dried-up rottenness –
> Let it crumble, let them twist!

And that was it. We wandered out on that Sunday morning down to the banks of the Warthe and talked about rivers, mountains, forests and clouds...

May came. Now we set out for a second time. But to where? None of the few hundred young officers knew yet, even when the bright white headlamps of our transport lit the way for us to the Schlesischer Bahnhof in Berlin. The future was full of secrets and adventures, and out of the darkness of the east, into which the lights on our transport-train was already biting, there rose the shadow of Hindenburg...

The train moved without a stop through the May night as if it wanted to conceal our route and the end of our journey. Only occasionally did a station-name flash past us, sharply lit up by the lights of the railway. We were heading eastwards. The shadow of Hindenburg grew and grew. A cool May morning rose, blue and gold over the lakes of East Prussia. Were we heading for Courland, were we heading for Poland? Whenever we made a guess, Ernst Wurche pointed repeatedly at the parts on his large-scale military map which were coloured in deep blue or light green. The brightness of a beloved May held out to the former *Wandervogel* rambler its tempting pictures of broad, sunlit lakes, shady woods and meadows wet with the dew.

At the station of a small East Prussian town, laughing girls handed refreshments and flowers into the compartment for us. As the train started to move again, with the people waving, calling out to us and laughing, an older man, with an almost angry look on his face, threw us a copy of a news extra. We caught it and read it. Italy had declared war on Austria...

For the past few days we had expected nothing else. There were not many of us who hadn't bet, while we were still in Berlin, that we ourselves would fetch up on the Italian front. And now the treachery of Italy was there before our eyes, like an ugly face. Everything was quiet for a while. Then there were loud, hard and strong words. One of

10

the youngest of us, who had not left the fifth form all that long before, stuck the paper on the end of his sword and waved it out of the window. A few girls waved their white arms cheerfully and boldly back. The old East Prussian in his black suit stood motionless and watched us go with an almost threatening look. The station disappeared behind us. The people on the platform got smaller. A few light and colourful spots and in the middle a black stripe… and then that disappeared as well. Only the news extra with its large, angry black print was still there on the red plush seats in our compartment. One after another we picked it up, and eventually it was screwed up and tossed into a corner. The conversation had long since moved on to other matters. A young university lecturer from Berlin, who had fought as a volunteer with one of the recently raised regiments in Flanders, told us about the hell of Ypres.

My glance fell by chance upon Ernst Wurche. He sat quietly in his corner, but his eyes were as bright and joyful as the May sun on the pages of a little book that lay open on his lap. It was his copy of the New Testament. "Are you dozing, little Ernst," I teased him, since he was so clearly disinclined to take part in our conversation. He looked up, frank and open. Then, with a quick and cheerful movement he passed me the little black volume and pointed at a verse. "He that dipped his hand with me in the dish, the same shall betray me," I read. I thought I understood him. "Italy?" I asked. He nodded, and pointed to another verse. "Then one of the twelve, who was called Judas Iscariot, went unto the chief priests and said, What are you willing to give me, and I will deliver him unto you?" I nodded, and he quickly turned over a couple of pages. "And this will be the end!" His finger rested on the pitiful words of the traitor: "I have sinned in that I betrayed innocent blood." And then: "But they said, What is that to us?

11

See thou to it!"

There was no trace in his open look and his cheerful gestures of a gloomy zealot. His soul was large and full of sunshine, and he read those Bible passages in exactly the same bright, strong spirit with which we looked up at the shining moon in God's heavens when we set out for France as volunteers. His Christianity was all strength and life. He found religious feelings if they were brought about by cowardice to be utterly pitiful. He had a quiet but heartfelt disgust for the fear-inspired Christianity and panicky prayers of cowards, something which was becoming increasingly common at the front and at home. He once said of people like that: "They are always trying to squeeze themselves into God's will. God's will is less holy to them than their own little scrap of life. You should always and only pray for strength. You should strive to take God's hand, not to scramble for a couple of coppers out of His hand." His God wore a sword, and his Christ also carried a shining sword when he strode with him into battle. Just now he saw that same clean blade raised against the former allies who had now betrayed us. His eyes were burning with it.

The young officer's religion was as unassailable as his commission. His faith and his honour belonged together. Later on I once heard a slightly older fellow-soldier make fun of his theology studies with a mocking remark. He looked straight at him and said in a calm and friendly tone: "Theology is something for clear thinkers, not for clots." He never lost his calmness, not even when he was being coarse, and he could be course if he wanted.

Gradually it became apparent where we were going. We spent one night in Suwalki, and on the next day the train – which now only had a few carriages – chugged through the endless pine-forests of Augustów to the front. One part of the track regularly came under Russian artillery-fire. We stopped for a few hours on an open stretch, while the enemy peppered the track up ahead with shells. The tops of trees broke off as if struck by lightning. Part of the forest was on fire, a sharp, hot redness eating through the heavy smoke of burning wood and resin.

After a while the enemy artillery became quiet and our train could move off again. Sand and fir-trees, fir-trees and sand flew past us faster and faster. And then suddenly the whole train was shaken by the thundering blast of an exploding shell, the whistling of which had gone unheard because of the rattle of the wheels. A crunching of wood and iron. A couple of jolts as if someone had punched hard through the red upholstery. One of the windows burst out of its frame with a sound like a whip-crack. The carriage heeled over hard to the right, wavered, and got its balance. The shell had hit the railway embankment and torn away the earth underneath the hot rails as if with a diabolical fist. The train had come off the lines and was standing at a dangerous incline over the steep drop of the hillside. The hammering of a machine-gun could be heard in the distance, from which point the direct hit had presumably been observed through the field-telescope. Tack-ta-tack-tack-tack-ta-tack…

Ernst Wurche had been standing by the window at the moment having a shave. The noise and mayhem happened when he was in mid-stroke. He removed the razor gently from his face and held onto the luggage-rack with his other hand. We watched our comrades in the neighbouring compartment jump down from the shaky train, some of them in their shirtsleeves. A case and a kitbag had landed on my head and thrown me forwards. I scrambled up. The train was standing still. I looked at Wurche and I had to laugh. He finished the interrupted razor-stroke, wiped the soap from his face and said placidly: "Oh well, I suppose we'd better get off now as well!" He never let anyone take away his cheerful and relaxed manner, and it was not in his nature to leave the barber-shop in panic with shaving-soap on his face, just so long as there was still time to wipe it off. Composure was one of his favourite words, and he saw it as essential to human and masculine dignity; a cheerful and relaxed assuredness shone out over his entire being, and it contains as much grace as dignity.

To be sure, the actual process of getting off was a little tricky. All the doors to the outside and to the neighbouring compartments were jammed. "Let's scale the walls!" said Wurche, and clambered through the blown-out window into the open. I threw our luggage after him, then came out the same way. We piled up our bags close to the side of the steep embankment that faced away from the enemy and stretched out next to them in the grass and the sunshine. Two hours later a relief train came from Augustów and took us with only a little delay to our destination. Russia had given us its welcome.

At division headquarters in Augustów we were assigned to regiments, and shortly afterwards, in a Russian barracks, to companies. Both times I was able to arrange it so that I stayed with Wurche. We were both sent to the Ninth Company of an Alsace infantry regiment.

We spent the night on straw in the Russian barracks, and the next morning walked out, four of us together on that day in May, to our company's trenches, which were a few hours' walk away in solid positions in the woods.

A morning dip in the "White Lake" gave a freshness to the whole day. Our route lay through sandy ground and fir-trees. Broken light fell in broad stripes through the green tree-tops and golden-red trunks. And then the wide lake lay there before us, itself bathed in the aura of the morning sun. Orioles made a chattering noise, swallows swooped down on the water, divers bobbed down and disappeared as we came

14

strolling along the shore. Only from the distance could we hear the dull rumbling, and from time to time the rhythmic hammering of machine-gun fire. "Woodpeckers!" laughed Wurche as he let the water and the sun over his body.

After that our path took us along the Augustów canal and the meadows alongside the River Netta. Soon the grey dust of the Russian country road was all over our tunics. But alongside the *Wandervogel*, as he marched with his helmet, sword and leather boots along the sandy road came the spirit of May itself, stepping lightly and cleanly through the still-damp grass of the meadows and smiling across to us ever more brightly. Soon the soft River Netta joined us on our way, and its eddies and the play of the mayflies in the sunshine entertained us, but then it moved away from us again and hid itself in the cow-parsley and the tall grass. I had been looking at Wurche for a long time, and in the end I had to laugh. "Admit it!" I said. "You will need another dip today, won't you?" "Right now!" he said, and we went out into the marshy, grassy meadow, threw off our dusty clothes and then gave ourselves up to the good, cool water.

After that we lay for a long time in the clean grass and let the wind and sun dry us. The last to come out of the water was our *Wandervogel*. The spring day was now fully awake, and echoing with birdsong in the sunshine. The young man who now stepped towards us was intoxicated with the spring. With his head thrown back he let the May sunshine flow over his body, he held everything still and stood with his arms outstretched and his hands open wide. From his lips came Goethe's passionate lines, which came freely and easily from his lips, as if he had somehow just now found those everlasting words, poured into him by the sun and pouring then out through his heart and his lips:

How in the morning brightness
Your glow is all around me,
Springtime, my beloved!
With what manifold raptures
There pierces to my heart
Your everlasting warmth,
A holy sense,
A never-ending beauty!
If I could only clasp you
In my arms!

Still wet from the river and glowing with the sun and with youth, the twenty-year-old stood there in his slim purity, and the words of Goethe's poem "Ganymede" came simply and beautifully from his lips with an almost painfully acute sense of longing. "We need an artist to paint him!" said someone. I said nothing, and felt almost melancholy without being able to tell why. But then our *Wandervogel* dropped his arms and with a few rapid and easy paces came amongst us. We shook the last drops of water from our hands and put our clothes on. Soon my friend was striding along again in his grey uniform, which fitted his tall figure neatly and well, his sword hanging at his side. The rim of his helmet surrounded the unusual shape of his interestingly elongated and finely-domed skull, and as he strode with a free and swinging step towards the woods, which echoed lightly with the distant thunder, he seemed to be listening with curiosity, trembling with anticipation and strength, to the sounds of the future. "If inspiration fails you not, then you can sing in rain and storms and hail…" And when his lips were not giving voice, you could hear it in his steps. "Young men must learn to dance, must learn to fight." Old phrases sprang up like fresh sources as we passed along the way.

How is it that all the beauty of life takes hold of us, rather than that we take hold of it? Oh, just as man is made of earth and to earth shall return, all beauty comes from longing and returns to it again. We chase after beauty until it becomes longing...

In the winter nights that we had spent in the trenches near Verdun, sometimes a sudden shout of Hurrah! would break out and go on rolling noisily along the endless front line of trenches like a flood-tide. When this shout died away in the distance, we volunteers would listen to it, and in this was a certain grimness and envy. In the east, everything was hot, wild and great. There hung over Russia a constant fiery red cloud, in which the thunderous name of Hindenburg rumbled, while for us in the west there was nothing left to do except to guard, to wait, to watch and to dig graves, although we never had death in front of us – it would sneak maliciously into our lines by day or by night. Out there in the east our columns were striding out over hills and dales, while we were lying up like moles under the ground, and shouting out Hurrah! to acclaim their victories.

When we arrived at the eastern front, the great battles for Masuria had atrophied into trench-warfare. Our new company had been dug in for weeks at the wooded edge of a large marshy area, through which a sluggish little stream, the Kolnizanka, slid through the sand and moors down to Lake Kolno. On the far side of that lazy stream were more fields, sand and forest, and over there only a couple of lighter strips showed where the enemy was waiting behind the sand-walls of their defences. There was a barbed-wire entanglement along the length of our front, and during the night the wire was electrified, the current provided by huge cables from Augustów. "Wire!" grumbled Lieutenant Wurche dismissively, when on the May evening after our arrival we walked along the company front-line for the first time, and he hit out mockingly against the shiny protective wire around the look-out post with a switch of wood. And so that first night we walked up and down along the grey entanglement like a captive tiger behind the bars of a cage.

Our sections of the trench were adjacent and we remained neighbours as commanders of the second and third platoons, or, as he put it, as "night watchmen for the Eastern Security Board". The Russian trenches were a few hundred yards away, so that even in broad daylight we were able to move about freely in the woods behind our position. To be sure, the Russian artillery did shower our trenches with shells and shrapnel from time to time, and once a direct hit even reduced my own dugout to rubble just as I was opening the door, but it always passed like rain in May, only a quick shower – the French were far better at this game, and by and large we didn't take "Ivan the Terrible", our name for the Russians, all that seriously. We did learn later to respect them, but for the moment we didn't let them disturb our "summer break in the Augustów woods". The thousands of mosquitoes that bred in the woods and marshes were far more of a problem for us than the Russians behind their wire.

Only when it began to get dark and the red, blue and multi-coloured blooms of campion, forget-me-nots, arum lilies and pinks out there in the marshy meadows grew pale and colourless under the stars and the Very lights, only then did Adventure, like some majestic stag, step out of the dark woods over there and gaze across at us as we stood listening by the parapet of our own dank trench. Every night a reconnaissance patrol under the command of an officer went out from

18

the company into no-man's-land and we three lieutenants, one from Mecklenburg, one from Silesia and one from Thuringia took turns in this duty. Sometimes two of us went out with our men, if we thought we might get an especially good catch. But usually only one went as leader, and it was always a strange feeling when you stood there by the parapet listening, and out there in the dark you heard the sudden rattle of Russian or German guns or the dull explosion of hand-grenades going off. The waiting and the welcoming back in those hours – of which nobody ever spoke – makes men grow together like intertwined trees. Not many words were exchanged, it is true: there was just a joke or a handshake when the other man went out or came back.

How could young hearts fail to become intertwined in those spring days and nights, in which we all became more and more familiar with the earth, the air and the water, with the gentle night hours and with the bright hours of the blossoming day! The memories of our first springtime of the war in the woods of Augustów come back to me like bright rays of sunshine, wherever I may be. The mild, young goodness that lived in a pair of bright, grey eyes and rang out warm and fresh in a lively human voice, that goodness broke like a strong and shining light through the windows of my soul, lighting up the dark places and bringing warmth where things were cool and full of shadows. How clearly can I hear to this day, and whenever I listen to the sounds of the past, the quick footstep of my friend. I can see him, slim and free-moving, as he comes through the door of my light, pinewood cabin, and I can see a young, living hand put some flowers under the little picture of my dead brother with a fresh and heartfelt gesture, in which you could sense nevertheless the quiet and decent reluctance of youth to reveal too much of its emotions! And it often seems to me as if I could hold back that beloved guest and chat with him about memories

19

of those bright days in which even the seriousness of the war gave way to play and pleasure. Can you remember, my friend, how we laughed at the first prisoner I ever took? I had gone unsuspectingly on a night patrol to the marshy stream in front of our trenches, where more than thirty dead Russians were still lying after the last attack, to collect the rifles from one of the supposedly dead soldiers. But it wasn't a dead soldier, but a chirpy and lively lad from Moscow who had belonged to a Russian patrol that had been escaping from us in the darkness. Without knowing it, we had cut him off from his comrades and he was trying to avoid us by getting down amongst the fallen soldiers and playing dead. When I tried to take his rifle he hit out at me, and the shock nearly knocked me over when this dead man suddenly raised his rifle in my direction. Just in time I managed to get my Mauser revolver out and put it to his head, so that he threw down his weapon and followed us back obediently. So that someone else could get a taste of the shock as well I pushed him, with his rifle, without knocking, into the dugout of the lieutenant in command of the first platoon, who was sitting happily with a bottle by his hand; but the lieutenant from Mecklenburg wasn't remotely disconcerted, but raised his full glass to the chap, who stood there grinning in an embarrassed manner. "Cheers, Ivan!" And with that, Ivan relaxed, and looked at the postcards which were decorating our wood-lined trench, stopped thoughtfully by a coloured picture of Hindenburg and said respectfully: "Ah, Khindenburrg!", waving his hands tirelessly around his Russian head, to give an indication of the imaginary size of the head of our fabled commander. When our people, laughing, asked him about his fellow-countryman, the Grand Duke Nicholas, he put his head in his hands like someone who was seriously ill and broke out coughing, to create a thoroughly frightening representation of the state of his own commander-in-chief...

And do you remember how the Russian patrol put up that nicely-painted placard one foggy night with the words: "Italiani – also make war!" in front of our wire entanglement? And how the night after our men put up an even more beautifully-painted sign with the answer "Italiani – also get bashed!" in one of the holes they had dug out so neatly for their own purposes, so that they spent the whole day furiously shooting at it?

Do you remember how we used to sit together in the dugout while the Russian artillery was aiming the heavy guns at our trench? How, because of the air pressure from the close impact of a heavy-calibre shell, our lamps used to go out three times after we had re-lit them a couple of times? And how the four of us would sit there in the dark and the glimmer of our cigarettes fell on the faces, and we laughed and said "Ivan's blowing the lamps out!"

Do you still remember all those things, my dear friend? And do you still remember how you built a massive bomb-proof dugout for two sections of your platoon out of hundreds of heavy fir-trunks and mountains of sand? And the way we gave our new building a dedicatory inscription over the door: "Blessed is he who closeth himself from the world without hatred"? And do you remember how you used to sing as you led the whole company across the meadows to the Netta to swim, and how you spent the whole afternoon playing around with us in the water? Do you still remember, old *Wandervogel*, how you persuaded the most reluctant of them to sing, and got the ones who were least keen on swimming to laugh in the water?

Do you remember the glow of the rotted wood in the forests all round our dark trenches? And how myriads of June-bugs turned the marshland between us and the enemy into a fairyland at night? And

21

how blue sparks from the electrified barbed-wire used to jump and twitch on the wet grass like the shimmering scales of a glittering snake crawling incessantly round and round through the grey entanglement, always ready with its fatal bite?

Do you remember how we used to ride our horses on a circular area in the light sand in a sunny clearing in the woods behind our trenches? How you wanted to learn to ride like a Cossack? You said that the seven noble arts of the new German youth were singing, hiking, gymnastics, swimming, fencing, dancing and riding...

And it's true, there was as much seriousness in your pleasure as there was pleasure in your seriousness! And anything you did with laughter was more than just a game. Everything that you said or did was a portion of life itself, and a clear, bright and composed will forged every element together to make a continuous work of art.

When the young leader went out on night-time patrols with his soldiers, a fresh and controlled will was always operating, firmly and tirelessly, on the men he commanded. If they looked like moving away from him in the darkness and under sudden fire from the Russians, he was able to compel them back to the point at which they had begun to stray on their own. But he himself was always the first one out, and the last to crawl back.

When the unsafe and shaky dugouts occupied by his platoon were to be replaced by new ones, he left work on his own until the last. He was always able to keep every hand at work without making a fuss, and without cursing and shouting. He took his part in the felling and transporting of the heavy tree-trunks and shared the work. He taught the men how to put up props and shore up foundation, dovetail roof-beams and make foliage covering, just as he had learned in France. Clean in soul and body himself, he inculcated in his men a delight in cleanliness and decent order, getting them accustomed to it unobtrusively and without talking about it much, but by direct action. The relaxation of his men was as important to him as their work, and as a young company officer he was able to ensure that the men got time off on Sundays. In his letters to his parents and his sister he was forever asking for books for his men to read when off-duty and he chose the books himself, based on his experiences in France as a soldier among soldiers.

Within a fortnight he knew the names and occupations of every man in his platoon, he knew if they were married and how many children they had, he knew the hopes and fears of every one of them, and he was able to loosen the tongue of even the most silent. "If you have the men's hearts," he said, "then discipline comes of its own accord."

Off duty, in the quiet hours of the evening, we would light the candles in the small paper lanterns in our wooden cabins and we would chat or read. Often the candles would burn down without our noticing it and the moon and stars broke in on us through the glass roof of my little summerhouse, that I had made entirely of slim, moss-covered pine-trunks.

Then Goethe's poems were brought to life, Zarathustra's defiant speeches resounded, or the beauty of the eternal words of the New Testament, that he liked to read out in Greek, would flow gently over us. In such hours there awoke in the soldier the young student of God, and his soul, wandering freely and lightly between the two worlds, went in pursuit of dark beauty and bright truth. "In our prayers we ought not to struggle with God, God ought to be struggling with us," he once said. "Prayer is an inner discussion with the divine element inside us, it is a discussion with God and a struggle with our human side for the readiness of our soul."

Being able to submit to the will of God and being able to take up arms against the human side is what gave grace and dignity to his being. He explained on another occasion what he meant by the readiness of the soul: "if it is the meaning and aim of human existence to look behind the appearances of humanity, then through the war we have more than our share of life. Few see more than we do out here at the front so many of the veils fall away, few see so much malice, cowardice, weakness, selfishness and vanity, few see so much dignity and silent inner nobility as we do. We can ask nothing more of life than that it reveals itself to us; no human demands can go beyond that. Life has given us much more than it does to most people; let us just wait calmly to see if it has any more demands to make of us."

In Nietzsche's Zarathustra he liked the winged thought that humanity is an object that has to be overcome. His soul was forever searching for the eternal. Even as regards his own nation he was not afraid to confront transitoriness. Human beings and nations were for him transient and eternal at the same time. For that reason he was especially fond of Gottfried Keller's story *The Banner of the Upright Seven*, with its incomparably beautiful and moving discussion by the Swiss citizens of the prospect of a far-off death and of what they would be leaving their nation. The clarity and appeal of this, the most beautiful of novellas, encouraged us and gladdened our hearts on countless occasions, and quickened the words of our own lips like a new wine. And when, in the middle of the bright images of spring, the thoughtful and balanced words of the master-narrator Gottfried Keller about the death of nations were heard, it was as if a dark, deep bell had begun to sound in the silence, carrying our hearts with it in its tones of eternity:

"Just as a man ought, when in the prime of his life, to think from time to time about his death, so too he should in a contemplative moment think about the inevitable end of his fatherland, so that he may love its present all the more fiercely; for all things on earth are transitory and subject to change. Or is it not true that greater nations than ours have passed away? Or do you wish to drag with you a prolonged existence, like the Wandering Jew, unable to die, the whipping-boy of all the newly arisen nations, even though he had buried the Egyptians, the Greeks and the Romans? No! A nation that is aware that one day it will no longer exist lives its days that much more fully, lives longer, and leaves behind it a worthy memory; because such a nation will not rest until it has brought forth and developed to the full all its capabilities, like a restless man, who orders his house before he dies. This is in my opinion, the most important thing. If the task of a nation has been resolved, then whether it lasts a few days longer or a few days less is irrelevant, because new worlds are already waiting at the doors of time! And so I admit that year after year, on sleepless nights or on lonely walks I give way to such thoughts and try to imagine what kind of national image will prevail in these mountains once we are no more? And every time I set about my work afterwards with that much greater eagerness, as if I could somehow by my efforts speed up the work of my nation, so that that future national image will include respect for our graves."

I can still see Ernst Wurche before me, as he lowered Keller's little book at this passage and stared dreamily out over its pages. "The one thing," he said, "from which you must hope your nation is spared, is a straw-death, an insignificant death. But almost all nations have died an insignificant death. The thought of the heroic death of a nation is no more terrible than that of the hard death of a human being. Only the process of dying is ugly, both with people and with nations. But when a

25

man has been fatally shot and his guts have been torn out, then nobody should look at him again. What happens then is ugly, and is no longer part of him. The greatness and beauty, the heroic life – these are all over. And it should be like that too, when a nation in full honour and greatness receives its death-blow – what comes after that is no part of anyone's life or being…" There was so much youth and bravery in his words that I wanted to take his hand and shake it firmly and heartily.

The deep-set honesty with which he experienced, saw and considered everything often made him almost comically angry when we glanced through one of those well-meaning books being churned out in such numbers, in which some famous publicist or other had gathered together his impressions of the German front-line. He was especially annoyed when he encountered things viewed through rose-tinted spectacles. "If only they would stop using phrases like the general heroism of the masses," he once said. "As if it would not sound just as good to speak more honestly, more calmly and with greater accuracy of the predominance of a sense of duty, of obedience and of loyalty amongst the people. Heroes are exceptions, otherwise there would be no need to talk about them at all." His sense of simplicity ran deep, and he hated overblown descriptions and phrases.

This distaste for superficiality could, depending upon circumstances, make him either monosyllabic or voluble. For that reason he rightly saw one-to-one conversations as the finest form of entertainment; no other forms gave comparable possibilities of plunging without artificiality into the clearest of the deeps. Many a cherished and thought-provoking word, given to me by the hand of youth in the depths of night, has stayed with me as a piece of my very heart. But none of them shines brighter than what he said in one night-time conversation, leaning against the parapet of his trench, about the spirit of the *Wandervogel* movement: "Stay pure and become mature – that is the finest and most difficult art of life".

The *Wandervogel* youth movement, and the Germanness and humanity which its spirit renewed was the thing that lay closest to his own heart, and the warmest pulses of his blood flowed around this great love. It seemed to him – as someone whose own body and soul had grown freely and equally to a natural beauty – that the best form of education was to let the young tree grow easily, left in peace, and only washing the leaves when necessary. He did not close his eyes to the occasional ugly deviations in the great youth movement. "However," he argued, "deviant growths usually come about when you pull at or knock on the young branches senselessly. If you restrain a sapling by tying it back it will grow unnaturally, even if it doesn't want to. If people didn't keep on poking their bony fingers into the finest and best elements of the developing soul, then its uninhibited naturalness, its finest bloom, its modesty would be damaged less often. Anyone who encourages the belligerence of youth makes them arrogant and loud, and anyone who handles them badly makes them unpleasant. Natural youth is always modest and decent and grateful for loving care; but anyone who sets out to educate without first awakening respect, should not be surprised if what he gets is hostility and malice."

The struggle of German youth for its right to be allowed to develop naturally was something that he pursued with the same inner passion as the conflict of nations, which for months had held him in its whirlpool. He regularly sent some of his pay as a lieutenant back home to the *Wandervogel* members at school and university. "After all, you need to help fill the war-chests of youth," he would laugh. And then he got letters with uneven writing and sloping lines, or he got copies of the yellow *Wandervogel*-magazine with its black silhouettes and colourful ramblers' diaries, and then when he was reading, you could see his very soul in his eyes. He even sent money to his brothers and sisters "to go rambling with", and all the time in his heart he would be listening out happily for the distant sounds of the young wanderers, singing as they rambled. And in his mind he watched, smiling, as his brothers and sisters with their hospitable parish priest carried a boat through the rosy light of a peaceful evening down to the broad and shimmering lake, and he gave his light, pleasant and mischievous laugh when the trumpet-call of the parish priest became in their young, believing eyes the soul of that peaceful evening, a mighty soul which made their small bodies tremble.

Other letters came, too, which left him quiet and monosyllabic, and made the waiting and watching behind the wire a misery for him. In Flanders and in Galicia foreign hands were sending his best-loved comrades to their graves. "I have so many good friends to avenge…" he once burst out grimly. "Avenge…?" I said. "Would you also want to be avenged?" He looked across at the Russian lines thoughtfully, with a furrowed brow, and then answered me slowly, churned up inside and pulling at the words. "No. Not me. But my friends…" Not me, but my friends… That is how two human hearts are brought together. I stood next to him and was silent. After a while he put his arm through mine, looked me closely and firmly in the eye and said:

"The sword my mother kissed now lies
Still at my side today.
Rivers and streams and fields and skies
Are calling me away! –

That's beautiful, isn't it, my friend!"

28

With that, his young heart passed the trial by ordeal over that which he thought good and beautiful. And at the same time it offered thanks and close brotherly friendship to another heart.

He gave more indications of his friendship than he ever expressed in words. He could open his own and another's heart in the same free and open trust, without pressure or exaggeration. I gave him as a present the first copy of my war-book *Sun and Shield*, and when he had read it all he said to me was: "I should like to get to know your mother, Flex. I can come and visit her after the war, can't I?"

Gradually the bitter-sweet springtime smell of old foliage and young earth had given way to the heavy air of the summer-hot marshland and waters that had lost their freshness. The young crows, which our men had picked out of their nests at the top of the pine-trees for their own amusement had long since turned into large birds, who walked imperiously and boldly along the top of our parapet with their wings stretched out, cawed at the sentries, pecked with their quick, hooked beaks at the shiny gun-barrels, or investigated the cooking-pots and tin mugs of the soldiers. Adders and copperheads sunned themselves in the warm sand on the lookout for frogs in the cool base of the trench. The damaged and much-cut forest gave off a strong smell of resin. The marshy meadows were resplendent, thick and green, and in the stretches of moor that had been dried out by the sun, the red lines of peat-fires could be seen in the white June nights. During the day the air shimmered and trembled in the sunshine, and sudden thunderstorms burst noisily over the waving tops of the pine-trees and then moved swiftly on.

From Galicia came the thunder of new and large-scale fighting, and into the giant limbs of Hindenburg's army, which had seemed to be frozen in an iron calm, came the need to stretch and move, until the whole endless eastern front roared with the noise of fierce battles. We were still lying up and waiting behind our barbed-wire defences, but now we were only waiting for the command to go into battle. On our nightly expeditions into enemy territory we had pinned up signs on the Russian wire reporting with malicious delight the fall of Przemysl and of Lemberg, and we knew that these reports would sooner or later lead to the signals for an attack here too.

But before the growing flood of the great battle took hold of us and carried us off in its swirling stream, we were granted a few more clear and happy days, the image of which shine out of the past like the shimmer of distant, beautiful, luminous, reflecting lakes. At the beginning of that July our company was withdrawn from the trenches deeper into the forest for five days' respite, and we spent them in huts or in tents. As chance would have it, my birthday fell during this time and my friend helped me celebrate it, not with full glasses and noisy songs, but in his own way, with sun, wood, water and the eternal beauty of fine words from former days, but which sounded rejuvenated and filled with a new soul on young lips. That weapon-free and cloudless day of celebration, the sixth of July, was a gift from his young heart to mine. When the sun was at its highest, we left the shade of the red pines and went down to the meadows by the River Netta. The sun illuminated the deep blue sky, which had been refreshed by rainstorms overnight, and mirrored with moist shine the shining meanders of the river and the shape of Lake Sajno, merging in the distance into steely blue. The light came through the sappy green of the burgeoning poplars and willows, and over the luscious grass of the broad pastures the air shimmered and trembled beneath the breath of the warmed earth. We threw off our clothes on the banks of the Netta and bathed. In long pulls we swam down with the current and then swam back upstream, so that the water rushed fresh and strong over our shoulders, and we dived in time and again from the wooden bridge, hot from the sun and burning on our feet, diving headfirst with a great leap into the river. We went downstream gently on our backs and then ran back on the lukewarm sand along the reedy bank. We let the wind and the sun dry us off as we lay amongst the many-coloured wild flowers of the meadows, and the light, shivering rays of the sun passed through the air and the sand and our bodies and left everything alive glowing with intoxicated power and all-embracing delight.

Flowers fill the meadow now
The wind sings passing by
The suns warmth fills me with its glow
Cool in it now I lie.

The sun's free fire sends its glow,
The furnace set by God;
Intense and through all things it flows,
Soul, body, heart and blood.

In that immeasurable shine
And in the blooms, I will
Forget death for a little time
That makes the whole earth chill.

Shine down upon us, sun, shine down
The world needs all your glow

Bloom summer-earth, bloom on, bloom on,
Oh, give us garlands now!

The thunder of the guns rumbled in the distance, the world of battle, from which we had escaped for a few hours, seemed distant and unreal as a dream. Our rifles were lying in the grass beneath our dusty clothes, but we gave them no thought. A large hawk was circling tirelessly above the broad, shimmering depths of the green pastures and the blue waters; our eyes followed the hawk as its narrow wings swung it in broad, mighty swoops and then it hovered idly. Was it the bird of prey that tore away the soul of the young man next to me and lifted it upwards to free and divine delight? The *Wandervogel*, who once in a German church had been blessed with the verse which matched his own fine soul "They that wait upon the Lord shall renew their strength; they shall mount up with wings as eagles!", that young student of God felt the wings of his soul grow with that eternal strength which "satisfieth thy mouth with good things; So that thy youth is renewed like the eagle", and freely and lightly he lifted himself and his friend high above the bright deeps of the colourful earth. The young man stood there, slim and bright on the blossoming earth, the sun passed shimmering through his lightly-spread hands, and from his lips, from which Goethe's word so often came, there flowed this time over this sun-drenched garden of God the ancient, holy music of King David's psalm:

"O Lord my God, thou art very great!
Thou art clothed with honour and majesty.
Who coverest thyself with light as with a garment;
Who stretchest out the heavens like a curtain:

Who layeth the beams of his chambers in the waters;
Who maketh the clouds his chariot;
Who walketh upon the wings of the wind:
Who maketh winds his messengers;
His ministers a flaming fire:
Who laid the foundations of the earth,
That it should not be moved for ever...
Let the glory of the Lord endure for ever;
Let the Lord rejoice in his works:
Who looketh on the earth and it trembleth...
I will sing unto the Lord as long as I live:
I will sing praise to my God while I have any being.
Let my meditation be sweet unto him:
I will rejoice in the Lord!"

The eternal song of praise from creation to its creator sounded over the mature earth, warmed in its deepest places. The melodiousness of the young voice embraced the clear wine of the eternal words like a resounding crystal goblet. The well-proportioned man in his youthful slimness stood there himself a veritable thank-offering of creation in the shining garden of God, and from young, fresh lips there came over earth and people a breath of religious springtime.

Over the broad pastures, free and unsaddled horses galloped fiercely. Mares and foals grazed on the water-meadows of the Netta. In the water and on the green banks of the river there were the light bodies of soldiers bathing, the bright broad stretches of the Netta were filled with foam and sunshine and easy laughter. The eternal beauty of God held sway over this broad Eden and illuminated like the sun the bright image of the young man...

33

Above the noise and glory of all the battles and victories the image of that hour shines out for me as the strongest impression ever made upon my soul and my senses in my whole life.

But that evening the very same man stood beside me once again in his field-grey uniform on a dark observation-post by a double-trunked pine, from which during the day our look-outs scanned the battlefield with their binoculars; and the red moon was mirrored on the polished steel of his broad sword. His right hand ran with slight nervousness along the blade, testing it, and the eye and his hand were pleased, as often before, by the Roman form of this naked weapon. With his head bent slightly forward he listened in the darkness to the Russian trenches, above which the watchful Very lights rose and fell. Behind the dark wooden huts of Obuchowizna burned the red glow of a peat fire, and clouds of black smoke rose into the torch-lit sky. Huddled in the darkness of the enormous pine tree, we talked about the battles we were about to face. "It must be good," said the young lieutenant by my side, "to take part in a real and full-scale surprise attack." And he fell silent again and looked down at the broad steel in his hands. Then suddenly he put his arm round my shoulder and held the bright sword before my eyes. "Isn't that beautiful, my friend! Isn't it?" Something like impatience and hunger were in his words, and I felt how his hot blood was hoping for the great battles. He stood there for a long time without moving, his lips slightly parted as the moonlight grew brighter and shone on the broad blade in his light hands, and he seemed to be listening for something strange, great and dangerous, something that was concealed in the darkness. As he looked so wakefully and eagerly into an immediate future that rang with weapons, he seemed to me the living embodiment of the young squire, standing in chivalric vigil over his weapons on the night before he receives his spurs.

I was reminded of this strange, dark hour when, just before Christmas, I visited the mother of my fallen friend in his old home. After a period of silence she asked me softly: "Before he died, did Ernst take part in a surprise attack?" I nodded. "Yes, at Warthi." She closed her eyes and leaved back in her chair. "That was his greatest wish," she said slowly and if, in her pain, she was pleased that he had achieved something he had long desired. A mother surely knows the deepest desire of her child. And it must have been a deep wish if she was still worried about its fulfilment after his death. Oh, mothers, you German mothers!

Do you now know – you who have experienced that day with me, the day I have told you about – do you now know what it means to be a wanderer between the two worlds?

In the last days of July one of the reserve regiments relieved us in the trenches by Augustów. With full and bold hearts we read the orders about our replacement. Even if it was still secret where we were marching to, we knew anyway that we were going into battle, that things were becoming serious. But we didn't want to march without a sound out of the woods we had come to love. In the course of an extended farewell patrol we bade a nocturnal farewell to the Russian muzhiks, with whom we had lived as enemies and neighbours. We took red and blue paper lanterns and long hooked poles from our dugouts and crept in the darkness across the Kolno and crawled up to the enemy entanglements. There we used trowels and soon made ourselves a barrier against bullets in the sand, hung the colourful lamps onto the poles, lit them and fixed them in deep holes. Someone gave a quiet order, and the bright lanterns swayed, glowing red and blue over the Russian wires, then were still in ceremonial splendour. At the same time there rose, sung by a dozen young voices, 'The Watch on the

35

Rhine', swelling out over the Russian trenches. The salvoes rattling across from the enemy darkness had little effect on the singers, safe behind their solid sand protection, apart from the fact that every so often one of them with a laugh would have to spit out some of the sand, which the bullets flying over the cover had whipped up and driven into his open mouth. The blue lamp went out and fell, shredded by some of the bullets, but the red lanterns held on all the more effectively as they swayed and flickered in the hail of gun-fire. Gradually, as the singing and the laughter went on unrestrainedly, the whole Russian side reacted; but the more angrily they shot from their trenches the more certainly we knew that no stronger patrol had been sent out against us in punishment for our night-time nonsense by their barbed wire. Very lights went up, hung there flickering for a while in their hovering brightness, sank down and went out smoking near us in the sand; they were greeted with a cheer, as an extra part of these nocturnal fireworks. Gradually the shooting died down, and it was getting on for the time for our little patrol to withdraw, before they were driven out by stronger Russian forces. This night-time nonsense couldn't be allowed to cost us anyone. But just as I was about to give the order to withdraw, one of the young volunteers turned to me in the sand as quick as lightning, looked at me and begged: "Lieutenant – what about the one about the musketeer?" And before I could answer him, ten or more voices joined in, vying with each other in their eagerness, with the words of the good old soldiers' song. I couldn't do anything about it. I gave way and limited myself to keeping a close eye on things, while the lads roared out verse after verse. I was a little relieved when the Russian gun-fire started again; clearly the Russians didn't feel too inclined to go out and actually collar the cheeky crew making so much noise under their noses. Even the longest song –

soldiers' songs included – come to an end. But my hopes proved false, because after the one about the musketeer it seemed that my grey-uniformed lads absolutely had to sing 'In the Midnight Hour'. "Lieutenant, sir – 'When I wait in the midnight hour!'…?" Just try and be cautious in the face of such school-boy jollity after twelve months of war! I stayed there lying on my front in the sand and laughed as my lads sang more and more vigorously and spat out more and more sand. Two red lanterns remained in place, amazingly, although they flickered and swung about. But everything has to come to an end, and I gave a firm no to all further suggestions for extending the programme, and had the men crawl back one at a time to the nearest point in the field where we could reassemble under cover. After another hundred years we jumped up and got ourselves across the brook. Luckily nobody was hit by the fond farewells that were whistling across behind us. Back in our trenches we were amused by the worried face of our company commander, who had already reported to the sub-section command post the presence of red signal-lights in the Russian trenches, and now listened to our patrol report in some bafflement. The cheeky joke did not really serve a purpose, but it was a good indication of the spirit of our men going off to actual fighting after weeks of inactivity.

The next day we expected our relief to arrive. Once again we went off in pairs, mosquito-protection under our forage caps, through the spicy scent of resin and the heavy smell of peat from the marshland woods down to the water-meadows of the Netta. Camped at the edge of the woods in hot sand, we listened to the mosquitoes buzzing and the woodpeckers hammering. The scolding chatter of the jays rang around our heads and the shimmering blue shine of their wings lit up as they flew up and down from clearing to clearing in awkward looping flight. The rollers, colourful as parrots, soared over the dank green of

37

the pines and the sun reflected off their colourful plumage. Far away, behind the steel shield that was Lake Sajno, violet fields of chicory and white carpets of meadows full of daisies could be seen dimly in the hazy sun on the horizon. The blue River Netta gurgled softly out through the vivid green and colourful wild flowers. Late in the evening came the rustle and rattle of the reserve company that was to relieve us as they marched in through the by now silent woods. Together with the dugouts and trenches, the reservists took possession from our riflemen at the same time of the live elements, the tame crows and the roller nestlings. Good wishes on all sides, and then our company left. In the darkness of the woods the company band, whose instruments were mostly ingenious constructions from tin cans and telephone wire, struck up with 'Honour and Glory to Germany' and group after group of the men joined in. Laughing and singing, we were off to an uncertain future.

We spent the night on straw paillasses in the Russian barracks at Augustów. In the next few days we went on through Suwalki to Kalvarja. On these early marches, which were quite a strain on the somewhat rusty bones and muscles of men who had been stuck in the trenches for months, our young *Wandervogel* proved himself to be very useful in helping the men along. Without much in the way of admonition, scolding or urging he was always able with a quick joke here and there to raise a drooping head, as he went up and down the marching column with a light and firm step. If one of the mounted officers offered him a horse during the march he always refused; as a platoon commander he marches with his men. It was not his style to urge on his tired group of men from the back of a horse to which he wasn't entitled. There was always something firm and formal in his step, which caused everyone to look at him admiringly. Not far from the town of Kalvarja the marching columns were spotted by the observers from the Russian artillery, and the explosion of bursting shrapnel shells swept over the short stretch of road they had seen. Shells landing hard by the columns as they moved along threw the black earth up as high as the treetops and dug out massive craters. To escape the bombardment the companies moved off into the marshland to the right of the road and continued out of sight though the fields towards the towers of Kalvarja. I can still see Ernst Wurche marching through the shellfire towards Kalvarja in the same calm and upright way that he had come down the steep slopes in Lorraine or had marched along by Polish lakes, or had come singing at the head of his company through the sunny wood of Augustów as they went to bathe. Nothing made him more hurried. The calm, firm, commanding step of the young lieutenant led the company in good order through the fire-zone and prevented the columns from splitting up in the unfamiliar and dangerous terrain. After hours of exhausting marching through swampy ground and difficult ridges the company moved again onto the main road. The lively step of the young leader rang on the stone pavements of Kalvarja alongside the slower forward movement of the weary mass of field-grey uniforms.

The regiment took up its permanent position again between Kalvarja and Mariampol, one set up by the Prussian reserve forces. There was a dreadful and foul smell hanging over the clay-walled trenches, in which dirty ground-water was always standing in deep pools and puddles. The water that seeped in was forever having to be drained out from beneath the flooring of the dugouts. On the far side of the parapet the slimy mud that had been thrown out formed itself into broad, permanent streams. In the air and under the ground the place was full of insects. Swarms of flies collected round every scrap of anything edible in black clouds, and from the support beams in the ceilings of the dugouts the ever-scurrying mice made bits of dry clay fall onto our heads and our plates. Ernst Wurche, who at this time had had to hand over command of the third platoon to a colleague who had held his commission longer, shared with me a narrow hole in the earth, in which we could just about manage to sleep on two bunk-beds, one above the other. When things got too bad we opened fire on the mice from both bunks with our revolvers in nocturnal offensives, which occasionally turned into furious large-scale bombardments. When we then played our pocket-torches like searchlights on that battlefield we lit up an empty area with the debris of splintered wood and clumps of clay beneath which once we even found the corpse of a mouse. The quality of the air in the cave we were sleeping in was neither improved nor diminished by the gun-smoke which covered the nocturnal battlefield. Otherwise we avoided as far as possible spending any time in that unappetising hole in the ground, in which we really did not feel very much at home, in spite of the fine and noble inscription which Wurche had set up over the door: "Second Platoon: Staff Quarters". At night we wandered along the trench and the line of listening posts, or we went out on patrol after Russian pickets. During the day we took advantage of every sunny moment to laze about or chat in a rather sparse flowery meadow behind the trenches. That flat field was the only clean space available to us in the wretched hinterland around Kalvarja, "Calvary, the town of the Passion". But it had the disadvantage that you could only spend time there lying down. If you dared to walk upright there, then gun-fire from the Russian trenches would soon be whistling around your ears. Nevertheless it was good to lie back on this flowery scrap of land, put your hands under your head and stare up into the blue, sun-warmed sky. It was while doing this that my friend and I had our last real talk with one another, and it was here that I was for the last time permitted to enjoy the whirling thoughts and lively images of his conversation... Goethe's poetry allowed us to forget the wretchedness of the surroundings, and often it was only the welcoming hail of fire that greeted us when we stood up that brought us back to reality.

In the early morning of August the nineteenth I had just relieved my friend, who had been on duty at night, when I received orders from the company commander to go out with a patrol to try and get an estimate of troop strength in the enemy trenches. The fighting around Kowno had made the enemy positions less sustainable every day, and it was above all else necessary for us to keep an eye out in case one day under cover of fog and darkness they decided of their own accord to abandon their trenches so that they could re-establish themselves in a better position further back.

I felt my way forward with a patrol split into two groups. It was already almost daylight, and at first I thought that we wouldn't get very far, because as soon as we swung ourselves onto the ramp over the top of the parapet a few shots from the other side whistled round our ears, proving to us that there was still activity in the Russian trench; besides, we should have to go almost the whole distance in full sight of the enemy. But strangely, the further forward we came, the more hesitant became the gun-fire from the opposite trench. There could be no doubt that we had long since been spotted. So either the Russians had abandoned their trench during the night and left only a few men behind to fire vigorously and keep up the pretence for as long as possible that the trench was occupied, men who, having seen what we were doing, thought it prudent not to annoy us too much in view of what might happen; or that they were trying to lure us onwards and

41

into a trap. In order to find out which of these alternatives was the more likely I took up a position with my two groups on a low elevation, fired a few salvoes across at the Russian trenches and then retreated a little way, as if we were heading back for our own lines. I said to myself that if the Russians were trying to lure us into a trap and saw that we had turned round after all, then they would let fire with all their artillery to finish us off before we could get away. But in spite of our apparent retreat there was still only a little gun-fire, with shots first from the right, then from the left, which went over our heads. Made confident by this, we turned back forcefully towards the Russian wire. At the same time I sent one man back to ask Lieutenant Wurche to follow us as rapidly as possible with a group armed with hand-grenades. My plan was to rendezvous with him in a burnt-out farmstead just in front of the Russian entanglements, then break into the Russian trench, and if were still ambushed, to get us out of any trap with hand-to-hand fighting. Everything went smoothly. On a pre-arranged signal we broke out from beneath some fire-blackened trees and pulled apart the knife-rests holding up the Russian wire. The eager and strong hands of our men had soon made a breach and we jumped over the parapet into the enemy trench. In that critical moment when we burst forward everyone's heart was beating that much faster – you could tell by the way the men grabbed at the barbed wire. Ernst Wurche and his hand-grenade group caught up with us in the Russian trench. A Russian sergeant surrendered with his group. We sent an orderly back to the company to report, disarmed the Russians and sent them, with two men covering them, after the messenger, who was now well ahead. We left some of our men behind to carry out further reconnaissance in that trench, and went with the rest of the patrol to investigate the second enemy position. We found the trenches on the commanding Hill 130 empty, and even the farmstead to the rear of it had been abandoned. It was only the extensive numbers of empty bottles in the bare rooms made it quite clear where the staff officers had been quartered. We sent a messenger back to the company from this position, too. We ourselves pressed on, unimpeded, for another mile or so towards Szeszupa, skirmished with a Cossack patrol, and established that the enemy had not stayed in the trenches along the sides of the river either. With that we had completed our assignment and we sent off to re-join the company. On the way back to our own trenches — we had with us a cart that we had commandeered to carry our things — we met between the first and second lines of Russian trenches some of our dragoons who had been sent in to clear up on the basis of our reports. Just after that we met infantry patrols and marching columns, and by the time we made our report to the company commander in person, parts of our field artillery were moving forward over wooden ramps out from our trenches. The whole division was on the move. Our men were beaming. The Ninth was the first company to establish the enemy withdrawal. Every man in the company was proud of this. We were sent ahead once again with a patrol to cover the crossing of the river at the Szeszupa bridge. But the bridge was already echoing with the marching columns of men, with the horses and with wheels. Cavalry and infantry patrols were already scouting well ahead. We threw off our clothes, swam in the river, and waited for the battalion. It would be months before we got another chance to bathe.

The sergeant that had been taken prisoner had said that his regiment had withdrawn further back and taken up a position by the railway line near Krasna. This information proved to be true. The withdrawal route taken by the enemy, the road on which we now

43

marched forwards, was covered in jettisoned cartridges and in places had been ripped up right or damaged across its breadth to hinder the movement of our artillery and vehicles. But the woods beside the road had enough tree-trunks for us to be able to make bridges across the gaps. In the forest, just before the elongated village of Warthi, the first Russian shrapnel shells exploded over the road along which our battalion was advancing. The companies moved in readiness for combat over to the left into the woods opposite the enemy positions and waited for the order to attack. Our artillery moved up and responded to the Russian fire. A couple of small farmsteads between us and the enemy went up in flames.

At the time we had marched out of our old position, Lieutenant Wurche had been given orders by regimental command to transfer to the Tenth Company. During the march he had stayed with us, but now, when the companies were separated for combat, he shook my hand and hurried off to report to his new company commander. He had been taciturn during the march. I completely understood. It irritated him to have to give up his people, his platoon. He felt exactly as an artist would feel if forced to give over to someone else a work he had already begun. He was enough of a soldier not to say too much about it. he was well able to distinguish between big and small matters. He took this small matter that affected him now no less seriously, but he didn't talk about it. And so it came about that we didn't spring into action side by side in our first battle. Two platoons of the Ninth Company, one of them mine, were deployed first. It wasn't much more than reconnaissance under arms. With the very first movement of our firing line, which had formed up behind the edge of the forest, into open terrain, the hail of Russian machine-gun fire rattled into us and made the first gaps in the line. I worked myself with my men in three

44

separate stages towards a ploughed field, which at least gave us some cover against flanking fire. The last step cost me one of my best group leaders, Corporal Begemann, who had on our patrol that very morning been one of the first to jump, lively and cheerful, into the Russian trench. Wounded were moaning in the furrows behind us. From our slight elevation we could look out over the Russian trenches. These were shrapnel-proof trenches, constructed over a period of weeks, behind deep, double-wire entanglements, a masterly chessboard of an installation, well-supplied with machine-guns, and designed to subject any attacker at any point to a devastating attack from flanking fire. It was completely impossible to overrun these emplacements by direct infantry attack without strong artillery preparation. To attack with just a couple of platoons was impossible. I gave the command "trenching tools!" and got my men to dig themselves in. Then I sent an orderly back with a report, and received orders to withdraw under cover of darkness to the other companies on the ridge. When it began to get dark we dug a grave in the front line for Corporal Begemann, who had fallen with a shot to the heart. His fellow-soldiers in the firing line knelt and took off their helmets while I said the Lord's Prayer out loud. A couple of Russian shrapnel shells burst noisily over the open grave. We filled in the grave, laid his helmet and bayonet on the low mound, and fired three rounds across at the Russian trenches as a salute. Then we withdrew to the ridge where the battalion was. Behind the burning farmhouses the companies were digging trenches and waiting, prepared for the next day.

No orders to attack came on the following day either. It was said that artillery reinforcements were being sent up as fast as possible to launch an attack on the enemy position.

On August the twenty-first, after two hours of artillery fire, there was an attack on the entire line. The battle of Krasna and Warthi has gone down as one of the bloodiest days in the history of the brigade.

Behind the bare slopes around Warthi the battalion formed up. The companies moved past the active gun-batteries and past the shallow indentations towards the ridge from which the attack was to be launched. Beyond this elevation there ran between burnt-out farmsteads a road that would have to be cross in the offensive, and which was under furious enemy machine-gun fire. The company advanced in platoons and groups across that road of death. I saw Lieutenant Wurche rush out with his group, rifle in hand, his head thrown back, with the Russian bullets cutting men down to the right and the left of him. Wounded men crawled back and stumbled down the ridge towards a dressing station. New fires flared up around Warthi and threw drifting clouds of smoke over the battlefield. Machine-guns hammered and stuttered. The gun-fire from the infantry rattled on. Heavy artillery tore into the air and the ground. The lines of men of the battalion disappeared in the terrain, melting into the meadows and the ploughed fields. Here and there a group would spring up and disappear again almost as quickly, as if swallowed up by the earth. The strong position of the enemy had suffered only a little under our artillery-fire. The machine-guns had not been knocked out. The very breadth of the area of attack, which came in addition under devastating flanking fire from well-defended surrounding elevations, cost us great losses. Parts of the battalion pressed close to the Russian wire, and the attack gained a few hundred yards, but it was impossible to get a full-strength line of attack in place before the Russian entanglements. The last of the reserves were not deployed. The firing lines that had pressed forward now dug themselves in on the battlefield. At dusk, orders came to the companies to dig in with continuous trenches on one of the ridges. It got dark. Very lights went up. Spades and pick-axes clattered. Groans and shouts came from the ploughed fields across which we had stormed. Stretcher-bearers went out and spread across the field with their equipment. The groups assembled in the rapidly constructed trenches, fashioned wooden crosses, and made wreaths of juniper and fir-branches. Graves grew from the dark earth and were closed over the dead of Warthi. From time to time there was a crashing noise as one of the burnt-out houses or barns collapsed. And time and again there was a whimpering, or a sharp scream. Those on sentry-duty went out in pairs or threes in the darkness. Patrols moved through the sentry-lines across towards the Russian trenches. All through the night the searching, the questions, and the silent discoveries went on...

Ernst Wurche was lying up with his men in the front line. Since his company commander had been hit right at the start of the battle, he had taken over the leadership of the Tenth Company in the middle of the attack. His signallers had laid connexions to the rear. In the middle of the night my friend called me on the field telephone. He asked after every single man in his old third platoon. I had listed the company's losses, and the day had also left gaps in the third platoon. For every wounded man he asked more questions than I was able to answer. He said nothing about how things had gone for him. "Good luck for tomorrow!" "Good night!" I hung up. Then I went over to the third platoon and passed on to the men the good wishes of my friend. The morning hung pale over the trenches and the graves...

The new day was spent with watching and entrenching. The word was that heavy artillery was being brought up. But the next night the Russians moved away further east, back to Olita. Early on August the thirteenth we pushed after them. On that march my platoon took the lead position. The whole way between Nowewloki, Warthi and

47

Solceniki endless lines of refugees passed our columns, Latvian farmers who had been driven out by the Russians, who were now trying to get back to their abandoned farmsteads behind the German lines with a parade of wretched carts on which they had their beds and household effects, and with what was left of their livestock and horses beside them. Only occasionally was there a shout or a burst of laughter back and forth between the columns of marching soldiers and the miserable assembly of women carrying heavy bundles, screaming children and the hurrying men in their caps or fur hats. The villages and farmsteads to which these displaced people were going back were now lying in ashes beneath burnt orchards and broken-down fences. The distant glow of their burning villages had seared itself onto the eyes of these homeless people and left them dulled. Away from the road, goats and sheep wandered bleating over the trampled fields, while barefooted lads with sticks and barking dogs ran shouting amongst them. Our march went on, past this migration of the dispossessed, through deserted villages of ancient, blackened wooden cottages with low-hanging, moss-covered thatched roofs and orchards that had been stripped, past new graves and past the ghostly and neglected Latvian churchyards with rough-hewn stone walls behind which reared up black, gigantic wooden crosses, like mysterious Golgathas, bare, deserted places of execution, avoided by all living things. Dead horses and abandoned wagons, scraps of uniform and cartridges were scattered everywhere on the road and the fields, the harvest trampled and driven over...

At the crossroads just before Zajle I was ordered to halt by a shout from the communications people. The battalion staff rode up to the front of the column, dismounted and studied the map by the side of the road. Despatch-riders brought orders. The march was to halt for today at the barriers by the Gilujice and Simno lakes. The company

48

commanders were called forward and given their orders for the night. The staff and two companies took up quarters on the Ludawka estate, the Ninth and Tenth Companies secured themselves with guards and sentries between the Buchianski marshes and Lake Simno. The officers stood around the major, who was sitting on the edge of the trench, bent over a map and despatch-forms. On the road from Zajle came a security patrol with a mob of vociferous, gesticulating farm boys; they were well-built, blond lads who had been in bed with no clothes, and only their soldiers' shirts had given them away.

Beneath the tall cross on the way to Zajle I saw my friend once again. He had been reconnoitring the road to Posiminicze, where he had been sent with a platoon of pickets. We talked about those killed at Warthi. I talked about one or the other of them, men whom I had seen fall in their first battle, after a fresh and heartfelt will to lead the way had been working on them tirelessly for many months. A leap forward, a rush – and then dead! And that one leap had cost so much labour and love. – "It was not just for that one leap," interrupted my friend, "but for the fact that he took it with his eyes and heart wide open, with the eyes of a man! And is that not enough?" I looked at him and was silent. I was silent out of delight, not because I disagreed. But he seemed to take it that way, and put his arm through mine. "Have you forgotten what you made your old Klaus von Krankow say in that Bismarck-story you wrote?" And he drew the words from his lively young memory: "In vain? Let things end as they will – you will not have cried out in jubilation 'Brandenburg, Brandenburg!' in vain. Hasn't the dead concept of Fatherland produced living beauty and great deeds? Have a thousand young people not, in a thousand hours of human life, refused to think of the trivial, the empty and the wicked, but have they not rather gone through their days and nights with warm and steadfast

49

hearts? Can we speak of a time being all in vain when it has produced works of art from that most miserable of materials, humanity, and revealed them to those who had to destroy them like barbarians."

At that moment I was called to the company commander and received orders to go on ahead with my platoon to Dembava and take up position there to sort out the establishing of pickets and sentries. As my men got their weapons ready, I jumped into the trench again and shook my friend's hand. "I'm on guard duty tonight at Posiminicze," he said, "why not come over for a hour?!" "I can't now, I've just been sent up ahead." "Oh in that case... but it's a pity." "Arms at the ready!" I marched off with the lead group, with the rest of the platoon following at a short distance. The slim, upright figure of my friend stood beneath the tall black cross of Zajle. "I'll be seeing you!" I shouted out to him. He stood still beneath the cross and raised his hand to the rim of his helmet...

Once the pickets and sentries had been set out, I returned with my platoon to the forward company at Zajle. I was sitting at a table in one of the rooms at a farm and was writing letters home. The company commander was asleep on a straw paillasse. The farmer's family were all in a gigantic wooden bed under a mound of brightly coloured bolsters. In the corner of the room, surrounded by packs and rifles, the signals-men were crowded round the telephone with what was left of a candle for light. Every so often the buzzer would sound and a distant, squeaky voice would deliver a message, which the telephonist repeated under his breath and wrote down. The air in the room, crowded as it was with people, was very stuffy. I got up and opened a window. Pale and hesitant, the stars were just beginning to appear in the sky. In front of the house you could hear the steps of the sentries. Behind me came, from time to time, the sleepy whimpering of a baby who was lying in a

Latvian cradle, a wooden box hanging from the ceiling by blackened ropes. The night air felt light and cool to me.

The buzzer of the telephone sounded again in the corner of the room. "Lieutenant, sir!" "Yes, what is it?" I turned round, not suspecting anything. The signaller handed me the receiver. The buzzer had sounded the long signal three times. It didn't concern me, then. Someone or other was talking to battalion HQ. But I took the receiver which the signaller thrust at me. Why was the man looking at me like that? I listened into the conversation. "Report from the picket guards in Posiminicze. Lieutenant Wurche badly wounded on a patrol by Lake Simno. Request transport…"

It was absolutely quiet in the room. The man at the telephone looked at me. I turned away. My thoughts were all over the place. I wanted to rush out of the room and get to Posiminicze… But I was on outpost duty. And out there my friend could be bleeding to death. I wasn't allowed to leave my post. "Oh in that case… but it's a pity!" Those farewell words beneath the cross at Zajle came to me suddenly in the silence. I clenched my teeth. Over and over again I heard those words, casual, not very meaningful words that mocked me now. "It's a pity… it's a pity!" And out there my friend was bleeding to death.

I took the hand-set again and called up the Tenth Company. The buzzer made a shrill noise. The company answered. But no further reports had come in from the guards. The wounded man was still out there. A vehicle was on its way to Posiminicze. That was all. "Call me as soon as you get more information!" "Yessir!" All done officially, calmly, indifferently and wearily as ever. I sat and waited. I stood up and walked up and down. The man in the corner followed me with his eyes. I went out of the room to be on my own. Every hour I called them on the field telephone. "No further reports, the men are still out

51

there." Always the same. And I was hardly an hour away on foot, and could not hurry over to find my friend. I stood on that dark street in Zajle, stared into the blackness over to the south-east and struggled with myself, and could no longer control my thoughts.

There was a knock on the window. "Lieutenant, sir!" I rushed into the room and grabbed the receiver. "Lieutenant Flex here!" "Tenth Company here. Lieutenant Wurche is dead."

I handed back the receiver with a comment. "Over and out!" shouted the signaller into the mouthpiece. Pointless, it was all pointless…

I stood once more under the pale sky. The houses around me were threatening, dark blocks. And the hours passed, one after the other.

I was only waiting for dawn. Then I got over to Polominicze as fast as I could. The company gave me two hours' leave. Then I would have to be back, ready to march off. Without a horse it would be impossible. I brought out an open-sided cart and my men got a couple of farm-nags in from the fields. I told the farmer to harness them up. But he made difficulties. He had no proper tackle. I tore out my pistol and threatened to shoot both the horses. The farmer and his wife threw themselves on the ground, wringing their hands and howling. I dragged him to his feet. "Ropes!" There were none. Only when I took aim at the horses did one of the adolescent lads bring some ropes from a barn. There was no time to lose. I had to see my friend once more. He had to be prepared for his final rest by the hand of someone who had loved him like a brother. The horses were roped up. I jumped up. I took with me a young volunteer who could draw a picture of the grave for his parents. Forwards! I whipped up the horses and hurtled across the fields to Posiminicze.

Then I was standing in front of the dead man and only now did I really know that Ernst Wurche was dead. My friend lay on his grey army coat in a bare room, lay there before me with his pure and proud face, having made the last and greatest sacrifice; and on his young features was the noble and ceremonial expression of the readiness of a purified soul and of submission to the will of God. But I felt torn, deprived of any clear thoughts. In front of the house, at the left of the door, I had seen an open grave which the men from his unit had dug.

Then I spoke to the soldiers who had gone out with him on that evening patrol. Ernst's task was to establish whether the trenches by the Simno lake-barriers were still occupied by Russians. Going forward, the patrol had come under fire from enemy shrapnel shells. It was impossible for the whole patrol to get without being seen to the positions that they were reconnoitring. But the young commander did not turn back without carrying out what he had been sent to do. He left his men behind, however. While they took cover and waited, he made a final attempt to get a look at the Russian trench. Since he was always used to going first, as platoon commander, he crept on alone, yard by yard and managed to get about a hundred and fifty yards further on. The trench was still occupied, though only by Cossack sentries, but as he crept forward the German officer was spotted by one of the Russians, who at once fired at him. A bullet hit him, opening a major artery and leading to his death in a very short time. His men got him out of the fire of the fleeing Cossacks. One of those carrying him asked: "Can you manage, Lieutenant?" He answered quite calmly: "Yes, very well." But then he became unconscious and died quietly and without complaint.

In front of that Latvian farmstead, where he had established their guard position, and on the hills around Lake Simno, I decorated a hero's grave for him. Two lime-trees close by would watch peacefully over the grave, the rustle of the woods close by and further over the sounds of the lake would care for him. In the surrounding gardens there was a profusion of sunflowers and summer blooms. The sunny young man should have a grave covered with the sun and its flowers. I dressed the bare earth with greenery and with the flowers. then I broke off a fine, large sunflower, took it into the house and placed it in his folded hands, still almost like a young boy's hands, which had so much liked to hold flowers. And I knelt before him, looked again and again into the ceremonially silent peace of his proud young face, and was ashamed of my own confusion of mind. But I could not shake off the wretched human sense of pain over the lonely death of my friend, in whose hand at his last hour had lain no other hand of someone who loved him.

But the longer I knelt there and looked at his pure and proud face, the more strongly there arose within me an anxious and inexplicable shyness. Something strange affected me, moving my friend away from me. Then my heart beat with a great influx of shame. He, who had been so close to God, how could he have died alone? A Bible verse occurred to me, from Jeremiah: "I am with thee to deliver thee, saith the Lord." No intruder could have disturbed the last great conversation on this earth, the coming together of just the two of them, of God and the man... And I had complained that he had died without a friend...

I did not, of course, understand that at that very moment, but the germ of it must have sunk into my soul, and bloomed more and more brightly in later memories. Death is the greatest experience of noble souls. When the tale of days on earth is done and those windows of the soul, the colour-loving eyes grow dark, like church windows at evening, the soul blooms with richness in the darkening holy temple of the dying body like the sacrament on the altar beneath the eternal flame, and is filled with the deep glow of eternity. And that is when human voices have to stop. Even the voices of friends…

You do not need to try and find out, or to long for someone's last words! If they are speaking to God, they are no longer speaking to men.

If only I had perceived that more clearly in that hour of farewell! I had my friend carried out and helped to lower him into that green-dressed grave under the lime-trees. I settled him for the sleep of heroes in full officer's uniform with helmet and sword. In his hand he had the sunflower, like a shining lance. Then I covered him with a tarpaulin. I said the Lord's Prayer over the open grave, although tears made me miss some words as I did so, and threw the first three handfuls of earth over him; then his batman did the same, and then the rest of the men. Then they filled in the grave and the mound grew. There is a sunflower on it, and a cross. On the cross is written: "Lieutenant Wurche. I-R 138. Fell for his Country, 23. 8. 1915."

The blade which he, ready in arms, had carried shining through his young life, lies close to his heart, like a salutation from the earth, fire and water of his homeland, forged from ores of German earth, hardened in German fire and tempered with German water.

"The sword my mother kissed now lies
 Still at my side today.
 Rivers and streams and fields and skies
 Are calling me away…"

Those lines, which he loved in life, are what he became in death.

As a final farewell I hung on the cross a wreath made of a hundred colourful flowers, for which his men had scoured all the gardens of the

Latvian farm-workers. White, satiny stock, red-gold bog-star, woody nightshade and sunflowers, the whole mature summer was in bloom over the young man's grave as I left.

Marching orders came by the field telephone. I had to gallop back to my company. The drawing of the grave made by the volunteer went with me in my pocket-book as we pursued the enemy further. We marched along the road which he had, with his patrol, so faithfully reconnoitred, at the cost of his life.

That evening we were facing the enemy again. Shrapnel and high explosive shells from the Russian field artillery came over grumbling and roaring, dragging whirlwinds behind them, against the farmsteads behind which we were looking for cover. I sat on a pack and wrote to my friend's parents on a couple of military message-cards. "Believe me, you will demonstrate the last act of love to him if you take his death in the manner it deserves, and as he would have wanted you to. May God let his brothers and sisters, of whom their brother so was so fond, grow up with his loyalty, bravery, and breadth and depth of soul!" But alas, as I wrote this, how far was I myself from that submission and bravery of heart that I was commending to others!

And more marches and battles, battles and marches... The town of Olita fell. At Preny we crossed the River Neman. Near Zwirdany we broke through the Russian barrier at Lake Daugi, after we had attacked during the day their positions on the heights at Tobolanka. On the shore of the River Mereczanka, with Orany in flames, we came under fire. Then we moved into the Wilia region with new battles. Every evening villages and barns on the horizon flamed and burned like torches, which told the retreating Russian forces how far the German columns had advanced. On our way, displaced local people milled about like shadows, with children, bundles and packs, around heavily shelled dwellings and trampled gardens. Dogs howled on abandoned and destroyed farms, cattle and horses appeared and then disappeared again. Indifferent and with tired eyes we saw all these shadowy images, which were there every day like sunrise and sunset, dull and desperate for sleep we listened to the cacophony of orders and shouts, and the groaning of wounded Russians – "Germanski, Germanski" – in the woods and the fields – Sleep! If we could only sleep!

The dim light in a broken-down stable in Winknobrosz kept me from the sharp, grey brightness of a wet and stormy September morning. The straw bedding on which I was lying under my grey great-coat, gave off the thin, sweetish smell of decay, and filled my rain-soaked and mud-caked clothes with a damp and steaming warmth. From the brown bodies of the two weary company horses with which I was sharing my dull and draughty quarters came a sweated vapour which hovered like a grey mist in the patches of light which broke through the holes in the wooden walls and the gaps in the thatching. Through the wide gaps and holes in the rough wooden door separating us from the wretched living-quarter of the Polish village smith, came the impatient noise of the telephonists and of the officers' orderlies, mixed in with tearful Polish and the occasions bursts of whimpering from a baby who was being rocked in a hanging cradle amidst all the poverty of that overcrowded room. The buzzer on the telephone sounded and sounded... Everything was like that evening in Zajle. Why were people and things always coming together time and again to re-form the tormenting image in one's memory, and haunting, turning every night into a night of death? Today, tomorrow... how many more times?

From the clammy folds of my coat as it lay over my knees there were two moving, glowing points of light, the radium-luminous hands on a small, flat steel pocket-watch, on which the hours on this rest-day after many weeks of battles and marches were passing, one after the other, grey and weary.

I looked at this little gleam of light, shining in the midst of so much wretchedness, and strained to listen to the ticking of the little watch. I held it up and thought that I could feel its tireless mechanism like the pulse of some living thing. I liked to persuade myself that it was a little piece of life, good and true beside me. For this little piece of pulsing clockwork had been wound up by the one hand that was more dear to me than all other human hands, but which now lay still, resting on the cool steel of a sword in the grave. Ernst Wurche's watch, which accompanied me through the encounters in the battle of the Neman and the struggle for Wilno was on its way back to his parents at home in Silesia... When I had hurried on the morning of that unhappy day after the night when he had fallen, the lips, pulse and heart of my friend had been silent for hours; but when the little watch came into my hand I felt the light, careful pulse of the mechanism that he had set going, like a little living fragment of his life, and I had, and kept for a moment the silly and emotional feeling that I was holding the dear heart of my friend in my hands.

Through all the hours and days I made every effort to understand better the watch's small, indefatigable voice, which had accompanied me ever since then, through battles and on the march. And it spoke to me and speaks to me still today: "You are living the hours of life of my dead owner, your friend, the hours that God demanded of him as a sacrifice. Do you realise? You are living out his time, do his work! He sleeps, you are awake, and I am allocating to you the hours of his waking life. A true comrade-in-arms will stand watch for another – that is what you should do for him! Look, I am carrying out faithfully the duty that he allocated to me, and you should be as loyal to him as I am, human as you are, and something more than we dead things, whose life comes only from you." The quiet little watch talked and talked, and its voice penetrated deeper and deeper into my heart... I wanted to do what it said and rise above my own pain. In the half-light I wrote these words:

In the East, where the sun takes to the skies,
In the East a young man sleeps,
His grave the most worthy in my eyes.
With torch and sword the young man lies,
Where a Cross its vigil keeps.

As a torch he has in his white hand
A sunflower gold as flame,
And there burns on that heroic mound
A sunflower like a fiery brand,
A torch lit to his fame.

The sword he gazed on with delight
Still glows, though it lies there cold;
It covers the sun-child's breast with light,
The sun shall be his badge of right
From that flower-lance of gold.

He was a guardian, pure in love,
Of the fire on Germany's hearth;
Now the halo of youth shines above,
A holy flame in the heroes' grove,

Over the bloodied earth.

The torch which burns his grave before
Let youth to youth pass on
Until morning and evening come no more,
And in dreaming peace or battle sore,
The last Germans are gone.

A fiery angel of the just
Sleeps the sleep of the brave.
But when worlds crumble into dust,
That lance of light he will take up,
Will pluck it from his grave.

No more in the choirs of dead held fast,
Shining he shall break free,
Come forth with torch and sword at last,
Light the German nation, when time is past,
Through the gates of eternity.

My pulse was racing. I stood up and went outside. The freshness of the open air flowed over me. My heart felt lighter than it had for a long time. Then – a rushing in the air, a wild cry as the rustle came closer, a flock of migrating wild geese was rushing high over Winknobroscz, flying south. Their shadows passed over me. A memory came upon me like a heavy hand. How long ago was it that that flock of geese had rustled over the war-torn woods of Verdun as they migrated north, over my friend and me?

Rush on, soar on, army of grey,
Rush northwards to the sea
When you fly south again some day,
Where and what shall we be!

We too are an army clad in grey,
We move at the Kaiser's call,
And if we must forever stay,
Sound our Amen in the fall.

Spring and summer turned into autumn. The grey geese were still migrating to the south. In the distance their flights were rushing over the lonely grave on the quiet heights around Lake Simno… I gazed after the migrating flock, but not for long. Something like a hand on my neck pressed me down. I went back into that Polish smithy and threw myself onto the straw.

Our onward march took us deeper and deeper into Russian territory. We drove guards-regiments from Moscow and St Petersburg out of their positions in the woods, set up pontoons to cross the River Wilia and came into the hell of Porakity as it burned, with the flood of Russian shell-fire coming over it, as we waited through the murderous hours without heavy weapons, the boiling light all around us. We dug ourselves in just before Ostrow and listened to the howling of the Russian hordes as they broke through burning Uljany and were repulsed again.

So deeply into Poland
We pushed with swords of steel,
And ever harder grew our hands,

Our hearts grew harder still.

Stolen from us were our free skies.
What took our joys and youth?
That came from all the blood that lies
In Poland's sand and earth.

We bear our banners on ahead,
Softly into the night.
The blood upon the path we tread
Is the red of dawn's new light.

Through Poland I would travel
Until my blood is fired.
That comes from digging graves and graves,
It makes the hands so tired.

With swords and battle-banners
Our laughter died away.
No matter; our grandchildren
Will laugh again one day.

The to and fro of marches and fighting went on. But the war is burning
down. After the battle of Wilno I led the remains of two companies
out, back behind the chain of Lithuanian lakes, where we were to dig
ourselves in.

... And again at the head of the company
My horse's tired steps resound;

I lead them through night-winds and trees;
Marching feet echo around.

The wood is like a hall of death
With wreaths withering on the graves;
The company is a great, grey stream,
Flowing weary, wave on wave.

Behind me that grey stream still flows
Through leaves, dust, snow and sand;
And as each wave upon wave goes,
It takes both sun and land.

The stream ebbs, flows, and ebbs again;
My heart is weary, sick today,
About those many sons of men
Who sank into that flood of grey.

The world is grey, the night is pale,
On my mount my head droops down.
I am dreaming now, in death's dark vale,
Of my stream's once-lively sound.

My horse steps on with even tread
The grey columns before.
Grey riders ride with me, dead men,
Whom once his saddle bore.

At night we withdrew behind the natural defences of the lake-barriers, dug trenches hurriedly and waited for the enemy to come on. Our men were digging in day and night. All around the lakes the Russian villages were burning, red-glowing funeral torches for the dying war. And again months of stagnation in the trenches, as before on the ridges of the Meuse near Verdun, and in the woods by Augustów. And yet it was all different. The warm summer nights lay behind us like a distant and beautiful dream, nights when we had chatted and sung when we were on watch. Now the walls of snow grew up round our caves in the earth. Biting east winds swept over the grey ice of the lakes and sent needle-sharp crystals whipping against eyes weary with watching. The nightly listening and waiting lasted for thirteen or fourteen hours each time as we kept watch on the eastern front.

> Lakes grey with ice,
> Moon on snow's glass,
> How long must I stride,
> My cold sword at my side?
> How long must we fight?
> Russian soil, alas!

> Watching alone
> In night and in snow.
> Ice cracks in the frost,
> The storm sings a harsh song.
> Peace, for which we long,
> Is banished and gone.

> The fire's flaming breath,
> Killing, hatred, death,

Through the whole earth have spread.
With cruel gestures of dread,
Peace is declared dead;
Bloodied hands have sworn that oath.

By frost and pain seared,
My own oath leaves me cheered,
It warms me like a fiery brand
Through sword and heart and hand!
However things may end,
Germany, I am prepared.

Time slipped through those winter nights as dully as a flame that eats its smoky way through damp beech-wood...

The gaps in the ranks left by military actions were filled by reinforcements from home. Recently trained militia and young recruits. The trench fills up with unknown faces and new field-grey tunics, which stick out curiously amongst the weather-beaten and faded uniforms of the old hands. And again weeks and weeks of digging in and watching, and in the snow and the rain all the tunics become alike. There are no more unknown faces in the trench. But those that have been lost do not come back. Only in the long grey nights do they return and speak to us. Discourse with the dead makes you monosyllabic or silent...

First I am stationed by the lakes, then come five full months' worth of watching and digging in, digging in and watching with my Sixth Company. Every night is as deep and dark as an abyss and full of unknown life. The days are pallid and short and are nothing more than a leaden sleep and a disturbed dream. The nights are a hidden existence in caves in the earth and dark trenches, wandering up and down by the stark, grey wires in flickering and transitory bursts of light, watching and waiting on parapets and fire-steps, crouching round a field telephone… And out of every other night there rises up, dark and oppressive before my too-wakeful senses, that one night, the night at Zajle… The buzzer on the field telephone sounds. The still surface of Lake Simno is shining. Distant shots rattle. The sentries go up and down… Oh, you nights, conjurers-up of the dead! The days, which wither like leaves, are a dream and a deception, and every night the darkness of the night of death is renewed over Lake Simno. I sit hunched over the flickering candle in my dugout and listen to the voices of the night, and I quarrel with fate. Every night, my friend, I experience your death! You and I are together in a house that is on fire, both charged with rescuing what belongs to our nation, only separated by thin walls, you and I. And you, my brother, burn to death in the room next to me and I cannot come to your aid… I sit hunched over and quarrel with fate. And yet I feel you near me. You are beside me and calm me down. I can hear your good, young voice.

"Being a lieutenant means *living* at the head of your men and showing them how, and how to die might indeed be a part of it." I raise my eyes and look about. His figure and his voice fade away. I turn up the collar of my greatcoat and go outside. And the Russian night freezes me once again. I wander up and down by the trenches and the listening-posts. On the ridge above the burned-out remains of the village, the high black crosses of the Latvian cemetery rear up in ghostly fashion. How often have we marched with our weary companies past these bare places of death at dawn or at dusk. They are all alike, like shadows, one like another. But from none of them comes a cooler frisson than that which comes from the sunflower-grave by Lake Simno. I stare at the crosses. A pale light is trickling out of the dark clouds in the east. It is time to go to sleep.

Every night is a threnody. Night-storms howl and shake my cabin, made out of wood and clay. My heart is a barn full of wild horses, a barn which is in flames. Stallions stamp their feet, holding-chains rattle...

Quiet nights slip by like ghosts. The coolness of morning rises, I look at the now-pallid candle-flame with eyes that have watched all night, and extinguish the light. Every night is a threnody. Fog has captured the morning is misty and stolen away its glow! Winter has come and its frost makes all the panes blind. My soul is as cold as a bare room. The windows are all frozen. Not a beam of light from the outside world can penetrate to me. I sit lonely behind frozen windows, my friend, and stare at your shadow, which fills the room...

And I quarrel with fate. But outside the light is increasing. And once again you are close to me and calm me down. "Come on, let's see if I'm not more alive than you! Look, I'm going over to the window and I'm putting my hand on the ice. It's thawing out under my hand. The first rays of bright sunlight are breaking through. I'm breathing cheerfully on the cold, blind ice – look how it melts away! Woods, towns and lakes where we used to wander about are looking in, dear faces are looking in from outside. Don't you want to call to them? Haven't we always been wanderers between the two worlds, my friend? Did we not become friends because it was in our very being? Why are you clinging so hard to the beautiful earth that is now my grave, and carrying it like a burden and a chain? You have to be as much at home here as there, or you will not be at home anywhere..." The day has become mighty and my heart wishes to be lightened and to believe.

Every night is a threnody. In my grey army coat I lean against the snowy parapet and look up at the pale stars in this winter desert. And my heart quarrels with fate. "We have grown old in our deeds and old towards our dead. Death was once young and profligate itself, but now it has grown old and miserly." But my friend has come quietly to my side, I don't know where from and I don't ask. His arm is in mine as it was in the trenches in the woods by Augustów. And he calms me: "You think that you are growing old and mature. Your deeds and the dead make you mature and keep you young. Life has become old and miserly, but death always stays the same. Don't you know about the eternal youth of the dead? As life grows older it should renew its youth according to God's will with the eternal youth of the dead. That is both the meaning and the riddle of death. Didn't you know that?"

I am silent. But my heart carries on the quarrel. And he does not take his arm from mine, and doesn't stop trying to calm me, softly, with a good and gentle eagerness. "A threnody is no way to celebrate the dead, my friend! Do you want to make your dead into ghosts or do you want to give us our rights to our homeland! We should like to come amongst you every hour of the day, without disturbing your laughter. Don't turn us into to ancient and serious shades, leave us the sweet air of cheerfulness which lay like a glow and a shine over our youthfulness! Give your dead their rights of homeland, O you living ones, so that we can be with you and stay with you in dark and in lighter hours. Don't weep for us, so that all our friends are afraid to talk about us! Ensure that our friends have the courage to chat and laugh about us. Give us the right to enjoy our homeland, just as we did in our lives!"

I am still silent, but I feel that my heart is entirely in his good hands. And his dear voice rings out and calms me again.

"Just as sweet and bitter juices ooze from a tree that has been cut into, poets bring forth sweet and bitter songs. God has cut into your heart. Sing, poet!"

"My friend, my friend, my soul chimes with yours again like a bell which rings in harmony with one of its fellows in the peal!"...

From the eastern sky a bright and liquid gold flows out over the dark clouds and the dark earth. There is a rosy shimmer in the young shoots at the top of the birches. A small cloud of fresh greenness is there everywhere in the tree-tops over the dark earth. The second spring of the war is beginning. The storm rolls over the graves in Poland.

> A wild wind blows from the west, the west,
> Wind of the homeland, God's own wind,
> That leaves the cross or wreath distressed,
> If a grave in Poland it should find.
> Then weeps that wild wind from the west:
> Alas for a German child!
> Why must Poland hold you fast?
> German earth is cool and mild,
> But not for you!
>
> The wild, west wind sings as it weeps:
> If I but could, if I but could,
> I'd hold you tightly in my keep,
> Just as a child's nursemaid should!
> I cannot, cannot, and to God I weep!
> If I but could, if I but could,
> I would have brought you, in night's deep,

A handful of the homeland's good
Earth to your grave!

A wild wind blows from the east, the east,
God's wind over the graves now runs:
Homeland, find comfort there at least,
That we remain your native sons...
Over every grave it blows from the east
The earth is kind. New-grown
Earth, from the homeland's earth and peace,
We are ourselves the earth of home,
Be not afraid!

An Afterword

by

Martin Flex

(1917)

Summer and winter came and went. Russian offensives were smashed against our defences. Unshaken, Germany's army of the eastern front held its trenches. And again for months on end, a silent watch behind the parapet and the wire.

The spring offensives of the fourth year of the war roared through the lands. In the east they did not fan the flames of war to a new heat. But over in France everything flared up, on the Aisne and near Arras. The combined forces of the western powers were attacking the German defences. Walter Flex could not stand being in the stagnation of the trench warfare in the east. He wanted to join the fighting on the western front:

"Together with a few comrades, including a splendid old major, I have volunteered for duty on the western front. The only difficulty for me in doing so was the thought of my mother, who knows nothing about it yet. Apart from that, you know my feelings. I haven't done so to make moral demands of others, but you have to apply things to yourself to give them life. At the start of the war the lust for adventure was often confused with idealism, and that inflexible and uncompromising idealism, in which lies the present and the future salvation of our nation, has become a rarity. You letter provides me with a welcome opportunity, which I take up gratefully, to declare myself to be of your mind, the more so as you touch on the state of mind in which I find myself, at this pivotal hour for our nation, when you write: "My soul is full of anxieties when I think of you." There is no need. Any anxiety would only be justified if had, by failing to put in my request for a transfer, disturbed for sentimental reasons the unity of thinking and doing. I am just as ready to volunteer in the war as I was at the start. This does not and never did come, as many suppose, from a nationalistic, but rather from a moral fanaticism. I propose and stand by moral demands, not nationalistic ones. What I have written about the "eternal German people" and about the world-saving mission of Germany has nothing to do with national egoism, but is a moral belief which can be realised just as well in the defeat or, as Ernst Wurche would have said, in the heroic death of a nation...

I have however always held to a clear limit of thought: I believe that the development of mankind reaches its most perfect form for the individual and his inner development in the nation, and that the patriotism of humanity demands a dissolution which sets personal egoism, which is tied down in the love of one's nation, free again and takes it back to its most naked form. My belief is that the German spirit in and after August 1914 reached a height which no nation has ever seen before. Happy the man who stood on this peak and no longer needed to climb down. Those who come after, in our nation and in others, will see this divine high-water mark above them on the shores along which they move forwards. That is my belief and my pride and my happiness, and it takes away from me any personal anxieties..."

His wish to be deployed in the decisive battles on the western front was not granted. He was ordered back to Berlin for several weeks. He eagerly followed from there the fate of his comrades-in-arms: his regiment was fighting near Tarnopol. He re-joined it in time to play a part in the taking of Riga. He wrote home with great delight: "I am so happy to have been permitted to be there." After Riga came Ösel. In the middle of the new preparations for the offensive he wrote:

"Of the comrades who went to the western front a few months ago hardly one survives. There were some very good people amongst them, and I would have happily gone with them. I can still see them at the station waving from the train as it left. "Pity you are not coming!" Erichson shouted to me, the colleague from Mecklenburg who at

Augustów made up the trio of platoon commanders in the Ninth Company with Wurche and me. Now he is buried by Verdun. If he had suspected that we should soon take Tarnopol and Riga, he would probably have stayed with us. Where should I be today if my transfer request had not been turned down? Chance, or something determined? I remain thankful for an equanimity in my heart that has never really been shaken. Not, of course, that I have ever had the feeling of being preferred or being given advantages over others – but I do have the calm, inner knowledge that everything which has happened to me or might still happen, is part of a living development, over which nothing dead has any power…"

On the Island of Ösel he was struck by a fatal bullet, on the very day that this letter reached his homeland. He had taken his Ninth Company to launch an attack on the village of Levala. The battle was coming to a victorious end. Uncertain as to whether to resist or surrender, the Russians were still in position near Peude. The platoon commander on his left goes forward and demands that they surrender. Russian officers declare the man a prisoner. He runs back with his rifle at the ready. "Lieutenant, they won't surrender!" Walter Flex has got hold of a Russian horse, and rides forward. A shot rings out and misses him. He pulls out his sword, which he has hanging from his saddle. With a naked sword he charges at the guns. Rifle-fire thunders at him. A bullet goes through his sword-hand and into his body, throwing him from the horse. His company attacks. The Russians put their hands up. They are taken prisoner. – The first words of the wounded man is to ask about the state of the battle. The answer allows him to sink back, satisfied.

His men take him to the nearest shelter. He is cheerful, too, when he reaches the military hospital. He gets his loyal lads to write a card for him: "My Dear Parents! I am dictating this because I have a slight wound on the index finger of my right hand. Otherwise I am very well. Do not worry about me. Many greetings! Your Walter."

On the next day, the birthday of his youngest brother, who had met a soldier's death before him, he died. At one with life and death, as with thought and deed, he went quietly into the greatest of all experiences, a sure-footed wanderer between the two worlds. —

That evening his regiment received their marching orders. In the hours of the night that they had left to them before setting off, his men gathered together for a quiet memorial service. They made wreaths themselves to offer a last farewell and thanks.

The regiment marched out. Nine men from his company remained behind. In the morning they buried him on the green island in the Baltic which had drunk of his heart's blood. Grey geese were rushing overhead, migrating south over the fresh earth.

He rests in German soil, where once stood the old Teutonic Order castle of Peude. Wreaths of oak-leaves, woven in love by his soldiers, decorate the cross and his grave. On the winds of the Baltic comes his last song, of the life-giving force of pure blood when it is spilt. The northern forests rustle on the hills.

> For Germany we met our death.
> Bloom, Germany, and be our wreath!
> The brother, firm behind the plough,
> Will serve as my memorial now.
> The mother in her baby's room
> Will be the flowers on my tomb.
> The lusty lad, the girl so lissom,
> In memory of me shall blossom.

Bloom, Germany, on my resting-place,
Young, strong and fine, a heroes' race.

Martin Flex
On the battlefield, November 1917

Walter Flex's German War-Novel

by

Brian Murdoch

Not only is the term "novel of the First World War" usually taken to mean 'anti-war novel', but it tends to be associated in particular with the surge of prose writings in the late 1920s and early 1930s in English, German and other languages which looked *back* on the war – Robert Graves, R. H. Mottram, Ernest Hemingway, Erich Maria Remarque, Adrienne Thomas, Arnold Zweig and many others are representative authors. Although a great deal of poetry appeared in print between 1914 and 1919, or was collected later if the poet had fallen in the war, fewer complete novels were written or published during the war. Diaries, although related, are a separate case. There were *some* early novels, of course. The most familiar include those by Henri Barbusse, *Le Feu* (*Under Fire*, 1917), Roland Dorgelès, *Les Croix de Bois* (*Wooden Crosses*, 1919), or Vicente Blasco Ibáñez, *Los cuatro jinetes del Apocalipsis* (*The Four Horsemen of the Apocalypse*, 1916). In English works by women come to mind: Rebecca West's *Return of the Soldier* (1918) and otherwise neglected texts like Rose Macaulay's *Non-Combatants and Others* (1916). As far as German is concerned, although most of the great retrospective novels of the Weimar Republic – Remarque's foremost amongst them – were translated into English and widely read, German material written in the war itself is by and large unknown, even though the work translated here was a best-seller in Germany over a period of many years down to 1945.

As translator of the most recent version of *All Quiet on the Western Front* I sometimes have to assure people not only that Remarque did indeed write in German and not English, but also that although the book's first-person narrative has an undeniable immediacy, it is a novel of 1929, and not a memoir of 1918 by an author who was actually killed in the war. In fact even contemporary critics sometimes failed to spot the fact that Remarque himself could not logically be identified with a first-person narrator who famously dies on the last page. A more real parallel is provided, however, by the short novel *Der Wanderer zwischen beiden Welten*, [The Wanderer between the Two Worlds], by Walter Flex (1887-1917), who actually *did* fall, not long after the writing of his book, again ostensibly a first-person memoir.

German prose writing during the war included, most predictably, propagandistic material such as a contribution to the popular Reclam Universal Library, easily carried little paper-covered texts, called *Unsere feldgrauen Helden* (Leipzig: Reclam 1915) [Our Heroes in Battledress], 'edited' by Robert Heymann allegedly from a diary, but in fact just a series of unlikely adventures, with battle scenes which are more excitement than reality. Oskar Kilian's *Im Felde* (Leipzig: Reclam, 1915) [On the Battlefield] in the same series contained "comic and serious tales of the war", and has a chapter on the delights of the trenches (*Schützengrabenfreuden*). To be fair, both also describe military hospitals, although the nurses and the recovery are somewhat idealised. More or less loaded, but still non-fictional reports of individual campaigns were also common (in fact on both sides). In Germany a little book on *Gallipoli* (Berlin: Scherl, 1916), for example, was credited to an unnamed officer on the staff of the German Commander-in-Chief at Gallipoli, and it sold well. It ended with the (fortunately) over-confident comment that "January 9, 1916 is… the day on which the might of Albion and its friends suffered its first mortal blow."

A rather different bestseller first published in 1916, but then in expanded versions right down to 1942, was a volume eventually called *Kriegsbriefe gefallener Studenten* [War-letters of Students who Fell], edited by Philipp Witkop (Munich: Müller, 1928). The 1916 original was called

Kriegsbriefe deutscher Studenten (Gotha: Perthes), the title used by A. F. Webb in his translation: *German Students' War Letters* (London: Methuen, 1929). The tone of the letters shifts as the war progresses. Similar in many respects to letters, too, although the question of intended audience is different, diaries were kept in great numbers by soldiers on all sides. Sometimes they were reworked later – Ernst Jünger's *In Stahlgewittern*, published in 1920 (and translated as *Storm of Steel*) is an example, and Vera Brittain's *Testament of Youth* (1933) is a rather different one, based on the diary published much later as *Chronicle of Youth* (1981). English-language war-time diaries and also collections of letters have, of course, been made available in print over the years and more recently in a major online project. In German we may mention the necessarily brief diary of the patriotic writer Hermann Löns, who was killed on 26 September 1914 at the age of forty-eight. He was treated with reverence by the Nazis, who reburied with great ceremony what is almost certainly someone else's body. His diary, initially enthusiastic, but which very soon started to reflect the grim realities of war, was discovered and published for the first time more than seventy years later in 1986: *Leben ist Sterben, Werden, Verderben; Das verschollene Kriegstagebuch*, ed. Karl-Heinz Janßen and Georg Stein (Kiel: Orion, 1986; expanded edition by Janßen, Frankfurt/M; Ullstein, 1988). The title given to it is from the diary itself – "Life is dying, becoming, decaying. The lost war-diary."

One German novel written during the war was Fritz von Unruh's *Opfergang* (Berlin: Eriss, 1919, also Frankfurt/M.: Societäts-Druckerei/Buchverlag 1925) [*The Way of Sacrifice*]. Written during the battle of Verdun and dated "im Felde, vor Verdun, Frühjahr 1916" [On the Battlefield, Verdun, Spring 1916] it was not, however, allowed by the censors to be published until after the war. It attempts to make sense of Verdun, but also looks at the war as a necessary agent for binding men together, linked with the desire for a rebirth of mankind out of the chaos, a central tenet of the expressionist movement of which Unruh was a part. It was translated into English by C. A. Macartney (New York: Knopf, 1928) but it remains a very difficult work both in style and content. In complete contrast with this, however, is another relevant work published first in 1916, but which became more celebrated after the war, when it was much reprinted: Gunther Plüschow's *Die Abenteuer des Fliegers von Tsingtau*, literally "The Adventures of the Tsingtau Pilot" (Berlin: Ullstein, 1916; by the time of the new edition in 1927 it had sold over half a million copies). This work *was* translated, though the English version focussed on another part of his adventures and was called *My Escape from Donington Hall* (1922). It is, of course, a book about the war, but even the 1927 introduction claims that it is not really a war-book, but a book of true adventures (the genuinely adventurous pilot-author was eventually killed in a 'plane-crash in Chile in 1931). War is presented as a sport.

One of the earliest serious war-novels, however – that is, one that both describes and also engages with the nature of the war, even if its attitudes are not ones that we might now accept – also published during the war is that by Walter Flex, who was killed at the age of thirty on the 16th of October, 1917 on the eastern front, at Peude on the Baltic island of Ösel, where he is buried (now Pöide and Saaremaa Island in Estonia). His youngest brother had been killed on the Marne at the start of the war. His book, *Der Wanderer zwischen beiden Welten – Ein Kriegserlebnis* (literally: "The Wanderer between both Worlds. A War Experience") was written in 1916 and seems to have appeared in 1916 or 1917, but it was published in its definitive form after his death, with an afterword by another brother, Martin Flex, itself signed "im Felde,

1917" [on the battlefield, 1917]. It is translated here from the most familiar edition, that published in Munich by Beck in 1918 and in very many later editions, and which sold in their thousands in hard covers and paperback. These editions carried on the cover a distinctive motif of stylised wild geese in flight towards the stars, a reference to a poem of Flex's included near the beginning of the work, and which was set to music, though the words needed some adaptation later to remove a reference to the Kaiser. The little book is in fact not unlike a diary, a direct first-person narrative, speculative, with some poems inserted, and with some indication of specific dates and places. It is subtitled "an experience, a memoir of the war". However, it puts in the foreground the (sometimes homoerotically expressed – the bathing scene has been commented upon) friendship between the narrator and a fellow officer, the younger former theology student Ernst Wurche. Given Flex's background and the period, the homoerotic elements would doubtless have been unconscious, and of course we cannot assess the reaction of the younger man in any case. Ernst Wurche had, however, been an enthusiastic member of the pre-war *Wandervogel* movement, a youth movement/ramblers' association, not entirely unlike the Scouts, and he fell in 1915. The novel documents and extols this friendship (and Flex's admiration) against a background of the fighting, with philosophical discussions on art, religion, and especially on the nature and effect of the war on the individual. Death in battle is put positively, and the (glorious) death of Ernst Wurche – whom the narrator addresses directly from time to time – is the central point of the work.

The author-narrator Walter Flex wrote a number of other different works, prose, verse and drama, some connected with the war, and his letters were also published. He gives Wurche a copy of a book of his, and at one point he even has Wurche cite from memory a piece of one of his own novellas back at him. The Munich firm of Beck published everything, including fragments, with a special memorial edition of it all in 1937, twenty years after his death, by which time *Der Wanderer* had celebrated its own half-million milestone with a special presentation edition. His surviving papers are now kept at the German Literary Archives in Marbach. The work as written by Flex in 1916 became – in what is now the standard text – something rather different once it had been contextualised by the memorialising afterword by Flex's brother. That afterword contains a second supposedly historical death-scene, that of Flex himself, patently embellished and romanticised to become an exemplary death, like Roland's at Roncesvalles, interpreted by his brother in the light of Flex's own writings, again with reference to the wild geese, for example. In fact, both Walter Flex on the death of Wurche, and Martin Flex on that of his brother remind us of the way Remarque presents the death of his narrator at the end of *All Quiet on the Western Front*, a death which is also interpreted for the reader by a new narrator-voice. The dead cannot, of course, speak for themselves.

The narrator of *Der Wanderer* is both Flex himself (there are references in the text to the narrator's *Kriegstagebuchblätter*, pages of his war diary), but also, and at the same time, what we may call his created narrative persona. Interest in the work is now largely historical, though his views of a moral, rather than a nationalistic patriotism are interesting. It is deliberately literary, philosophical, sometimes stylistically rather stiff, sometimes a little gushing, with various overworked adjectives – *hell*, bright, is just one of them. The enigmatic title – referring literally to "both worlds," rather than to (any) "two worlds" – may allude to two similarly-titled poems by Goethe, one of which contrasts nature and the ancient world, but the other of which balances heart and mind as equal influences. Goethe's poems are quite often addressed to *Wand(e)rer*, wanderers, wayfarers, travellers, and other such poems are cited here, as when Wurche calms the narrator down over some petty irritation with a quatrain from *Wandrers Gemütsruhe* [Wanderer's Equanimity]. However, it is possible to interpret the title in other ways (quite apart from the verbal link to the *Wandervogel* movement), and Flex both uses the phrase in general terms (once in the context of Wurche as soldier and theologian, between the material and the spiritual world), and also actually asks the reader at one point, where the contrast seems to be between peace and war, if the title is clear. Towards the end, however, it seems to be between the worlds of the living and of the dead. To be *and* not to be. Beside Goethe, both Nietzsche and the Bible (Wurche's Christianity is thoroughly muscular) are invoked in the course of the work, and there are allusions to other classical German works – the description of Wurche's combination of grace and dignity, for example, echoes Schiller's treatise *Über Anmut und Würde*. The book is nationalistic in a not unfamiliar general-patriotic sense, ending with a poem about a grave and the *Heimaterde*, the soil of the homeland, showing us – *pace* one of our own best-known war poets – some corner of a Polish field that is for ever Germany. Flex and Rupert Brooke are eminently comparable in various respects. Its more general patriotism is underlined in a lengthy quotation from a work by the nineteenth-century *Swiss* writer, Gottfried Keller, set in his own country.

Although the fame of Flex's work was ultimately (and rightly) eclipsed by the Weimar anti-war novels by writers like Remarque, those writers were themselves nevertheless influenced by its individualistic directness and the stress on comradeship, which must not, however, be misinterpreted as a justification *for* the war, rather than simply being the one good thing that came *from* it. I have noted in a study of the work that it appears as if Remarque, when writing the most celebrated war-novel of all, took some of the features of this book and reworked them from an anti-war perspective. The attitude towards the war, on the other hand, is positive, thanking God for matching them with the hour; Flex's scenes of the actual fighting can be vivid, but there is always a feeling that they have been sanitised, and his heroes die too cleanly. In fact the idea is expressed openly in the work that while the fact of dying in battle is important, it is not appropriate to discuss the actual details, as the Weimar novelists so memorably did. The few glimpses of the actual enemy (on the eastern front), too, are not much more than either sketch or (earlier on) caricature. Flex's descriptions of the contrasts between action and the long periods of inaction are, on the other hand, more natural.

Flex's novel is a highly personal work, and such writing is always open to a wide range of interpretation. On one level, it clearly did appeal to those who needed to be reassured that the sacrifices of the war were somehow worth it, just as Remarque's work makes very clear that they were not. As an aside, Flex's publisher, Beck, also produced in the early 1920s, a *Trostbuch für Kriegsleidtragende*, a book of comfort for those suffering because of the war, called *Die Herzen hoch!* [Lift up your Hearts!] and billed as being "by a German mother". It is highly significant that in the ranking list of best-selling war-books in Germany before the second world war, Flex's novel is in second place, immediately after *Im Westen nichts Neues*, with the third place taken by Plüschow's adventures as a pilot in Tsingtau. Thus Remarque's retrospective and clearly anti-war novel, which is firmly against heroics and against the idea of war as an adventure, was joined in a trio of best-sellers by Flex, who *does* see death in battle as heroic, and also by the *Boys'-Own-Paper* adventurousness of the real-life German Biggles. All three reflect possible responses to the war, and the popularity of all three before the Second World War is understandable. Flex's overt philosophising and literary quotations were aimed at an audience different from that of Remarque or from the adventure-seekers who read Plüschow, but statistically, one presumes, there must have been plenty of people who bought and read all three. It was a waste of life. It was fine and noble. It was a game.

The attention paid to the work by the Nazis – extracts were read out when the announcement was made of Hitler's own rather less than heroic death – has presumably contributed to its present neglect. It is not hard to see the appeal it held for the Nazi movement and how easily they could exploit it. But the reaction of the youth of 1914 (and the *Wandervogel* movement in particular) to the stultifying rigidity of pre-war Germany in the desire to strive for a new order is by no means a foreshadowing of Hitler's brand of supremacist nationalism. The highlighting of purity, art, endeavour and friendship is as important as the patriotism, which is presented in a form common to all sides in the conflict, including the privilege of *pro patria mori*.

Of the Weimar anti-war novelists, Remarque alluded, I think quite deliberately, in his far less familiar sequel to *All Quiet on the Western Front*, a novel called *Der Weg zurück* (*The Road Back*, 1931), to Flex's motif of the wild geese and to the *Wandervogel* youth movement. In fact Remarque concludes his second war-novel – written not too long before Hitler came to power – with some almost elegiac regrets on the part of some ex-soldiers that the more or less harmless pre-war movement of which Flex was such a great proponent, with its quasi-ecological brand of (fairly local) patriotism, had been replaced already in the immediate post-war years by the new and belligerent right-wing militaristic movements from the *Freikorps* down, eventually, to the

Hitler Youth, and of course to another war.

The translation is from a soft-cover edition with the imprint Oskar Beck (C. H. Beck), Munich, 1922 (210-215th thousand). The title refers to the wanderer between "beiden Welten", rather than "zwei Welten", 'both worlds', rather than a more generalised 'two worlds', which implies that there are just two quite specific worlds in Flex's mind, although he leaves the proper interpretation up to the reader. For that reason I have placed a second definite article in the title. Even the verb "to wander" (much used by Flex) has different overtones in English, whereas in German it is firmly linked with the Romantic movement in the nineteenth century, implying in some ways a kind of deliberate and free-spirited aimlessness. Given Flex's allusions to wanderers, it is simply unfortunate that the medieval legend of *der ewige Jude*, the eternal Jew, referred to at one point, is known as 'the Wandering Jew' in English. The *Wandervogel* movement itself, finally, cannot be translated, in spite of the links with the title of the work itself and with Flex's poem of the wild geese, either in terms of migrating birds, or indeed (for other reasons) of happy wanderers, ramblers' associations, youth hostellers or the Scout movement; so it must perforce be left as it is, especially as Flex uses it as a tag for Wurche himself. However, I have avoided the plural form, which referred to its members collectively and to the movement itself – *Wandervögel* – because it might well not be recognised as such.

I have tried to render the poetry – Flex's own and that of others

87

cited (notably Goethe) – into verse, and translations of other literary quotations are also my own. For Psalm CIV, however, as also with other biblical passages, I have used the Revised Version, since Flex uses a modernised Luther Bible (and no two translations of the Psalms are ever quite alike anyway). Place-names are always a problem, especially here, where much of the (historical) action takes place in eastern Europe, in the much contested areas around East Prussia, Poland and the Baltic states. I have kept mostly, though not completely consistently, to the German or Polish forms of the names used in the work, so as not to inject too much modernity, which references to Wroclaw, Saarema, Poznan, Lvov (or Lviv) rather than Breslau, Ösel, Posen or Lemberg might have done. In fact many of the places involved are small and hard to find, even with the benefits of Google Earth. The place-names in the area of Suwalki/Suwalkija and beyond were affected anyway by the Polish-Lithuanian conflict of 1919/20, and they may now be in Poland, Lithuania, Latvia or Belarus. The name Kalvar(i)ja – Calvary – is at least still recognisable as an allusion. Even larger places, such as Courland (Kurland, once associated with the Teutonic Knights, now part of Latvia), may no longer mean much in English.

Further Reading

The work is still in print in German, and the original text is readily available on-line in more than one place, albeit in so-called 'Gothic type,' *Fraktur* (the 1937 memorial edition was even advertised as being hand-set in an especially decorative *Fraktur*-typeface). The best presentation and analysis of the work in German is by Hans Wagener, "Wandervogel und Flammenengel. Walter Flex, *Der Wanderer zwischen*

88

beiden Welten. Ein Kriegserlebnis (1916)," in the collection *Von Richthofen bis Remarque: Deutschsprachige Prosa zum I. Weltkrieg*, edited by Thomas F. Schneider and Hans Wagener (Amsterdam and New York: Rodopi, 2003), pp. 17-30. There is not a great deal on Walter Flex in English, but see Brian Murdoch, "War and the Bestsellers: Walter Flex and Erich Maria Remarque," in another large collection, *Heroisches Elend*, edited by Gislinde Seybert and Thomas Stauder (Frankfurt: Peter Lang, 2013), vol. II, pp. 1211-1225 (a simple misreading led me in that paper to upgrade the Russian Commander-in-Chief, Grand Duke Nicholas, to their Supreme Commander, Tsar Nicholas, and I may perhaps be allowed to correct that slip here!). There is some material on Flex in Wolfgang G. Natter's *Literature at War, 1914-1940. Representing the "Time of Greatness" in Germany* (New Haven and London: Yale University Press, 1999), and in Robert Wohl's *The Generation of 1914* (London: Weidenfeld and Nicolson, 1980), where there is a chapter entitled "Wanderers between Two Worlds." Brief but pertinent comments on Flex and the *Wandervogel* movement are made by Ann P. Linder, *Princes of the Trenches. Narrating the German Experience of the First World War* (Columbia SC: Camden House 1996), and the standard study in English on the *Wandervogel* movement in detail, where it came from and what followed it, is that by Peter D. Stachura, *The German Youth Movement 1900-1945* (London: Macmillan, 1981). There is a good entry on Flex in French available on the *Theatrum Belli* website (www.theatrum-belli.com/tag/wandervogel), with a piece dated 31 December 2006 and the significant title "une éthique du sacrifice au-delà de tous les égoïsmes".

Printed in Great Britain
by Amazon

36839682R00057